a mother's gift

a
mother's
gift

a novel by

britney
& lynne
spears

B◧XTREE

First published 2001 by Delacorte Press
an imprint of Random House Children's Books
a division of Random House Inc., New York

First published in Great Britain 2001 by Boxtree
an imprint of Macmillan Publishers Ltd
25 Eccleston Place, London SW1W 9NF
Basingstoke and Oxford
Associated companies throughout the world
www.macmillan.com

ISBN 0 7522 2021 7

A CIP catalogue record for this book is available from
the British Library.

Book design by Liney Li
Printed and bound in Great Britain by Mackays of Chatham PLC,
Chatham, Kent

To my daughter Britney.
My very special thanks to you for giving me
so much of your very valuable time to make
this story complete.

L.

To my mom.
This will be another memory
we add to our list of experiences together.
Thanks for your guidance, love, friendship,
and sense of humor.

B.

acknowledgments

We'd like to thank everyone who helped make our dream of writing a book together a reality. Thanks to Jamie, Bryan, and Jamie Lynn for always being there, and to Reggie, Sandra, Laura Lynne, Jill, Kelly, Courtney, Jansen, and all our loving family and friends in Kentwood and throughout the world; Larry, Johnny, Fe, Big Rob, Theresa, Renee, Bert, David, Dean, Kim, Lisa, Dan, and Mark—you know we couldn't have done this without you! With special thanks to our amazing editors, Beverly Horowitz and Wendy Loggia, and John Adamo, Paula Breen, Kathy Dunn, Saho Fujii, Judith Haut, Liney Li, Erica Moroz, Pete Muller, Janet Parker, Barbara Perris, Rebecca Price, Tamar Schwartz, Audrey Sclater, Andrew Smith, Naná Stoelzle, and Craig Virden at Delacorte Press, along with Claire Giobbe and Matthew Miller . . . y'all have knocked yourselves out and we really appreciate it.

Beautiful faces are they that wear
The light of a pleasant spirit there.

—*McGuffey's Second Reader*

chapter one

Gossip is the first language in small Southern towns. Biscay, Mississippi, is no exception. Gossip drifts through the schoolyards in whispers and giggles and seeps through the coffee shops and steepled churches. Gossip makes the world go round in Biscay.

Biscay is an itsy-bitsy little place, only ten thousand folks or so. "Biscay is definitely dead" is the usual declaration of anyone under sixteen.

And they're kind of right.

Biscay's only connection to a highway isn't concrete, but two lanes of grooved asphalt with chuckholes deep enough to rupture a glass-belted radial tire. That old road is the reason that no fast-food chain will ever open up in Biscay. There won't even be one of those major service stations with a food mart and self-service gasoline pumps with slots for credit cards. The biggest business in town, the post office, is the only reason Biscay is even a legal township. There's no shopping mall in Biscay. You have to take two buses all the way over to Hattiesburg for that.

Kids who grow up in Biscay don't have much opportunity. Some of them quit school early so they can help their parents farm. A few manage to go away to college. But most of them stay there. Get a job. Get married. Get older.

Life doesn't change much in Biscay.

One thing Biscay does have is a whispered secret, a nasty rumor that makes mamas shush their children when they mention it. It's pathetic, most agree, that the biggest thing that ever happened in Biscay is the one thing the town wants to forget. People say that once, a terrible thing happened, and people died.

That's about all the townspeople will tell strangers. And they tell only those who ask and ask at least twice about the mysterious plot of burned earth still sitting ugly at the edge of Biscay. Maybe, just maybe, the emotional wounds that still run deep will eventually heal.

At least everyone hopes they will.

Because people are people, with hopes and dreams and faith in their hearts and stars in their eyes . . . even those who were born in Biscay, Mississippi.

• • •

"Here it comes, Mama," fourteen-year-old Holly Faye Lovell said, bumping the side of the old television set with a practiced hip. The fuzzy gray screen blipped out, then blinked back in wavering color. Holly dropped next to her mother on the saggy yet comfortable old brown couch as the familiar toe-tapping notes of *The Haverty Talent Hour*'s theme song drifted through the small ranch house.

Holly's mother, Wanda, reached for some hot buttered popcorn from the bowl on the coffee table. "I wonder what we'll see tonight."

Holly grinned. Her mom said the same thing every week.

Everyone in Biscay watched *The Haverty Talent Hour.* It was like a local law or something. Holly thought she'd probably fallen in love with music even before she could walk—her mother had always made sure music was a part of their lives. They woke up to Elvis (born in Tupelo, Mississippi, thank you very much), spent the day bopping along with the Top 40, and drifted off to sleep with some easy listening.

And they had a regular Friday-night rendezvous in front of the TV.

"Sorry, I've got a date tonight," Holly used to tell Tyler Norwood when he had first started asking her to come hang out at the Ten Pin Lanes with his group of friends on Fridays. His face would crumple up each time when she turned him down, and finally she couldn't keep a straight face any longer and had to tell him the truth—her big date was her mom.

The famous Haverty School of Music and the Performing Arts, located in Hattiesburg, televised a weekly show featuring its best students of music and performance. Each week there was something different. Wanda loved the abbreviated operas, which always brought a smile to her pretty red lips. Neither of them was a huge opera fan (why didn't singers who were smart enough to learn a foreign language sing in English so listeners could understand them, Holly always wanted to know), but they would both sit in awed silence when one of the students attempted an aria and clap wildly when he or she pulled it off.

Holly loved it when someone chose to perform an old gospel song, letting the emotional power of the words rush over her. She was a fan of country music too, although she could do without songs about people feeling sorry for themselves, songs about getting your foot run over at the bus stop or about how your husband ran off with your best friend and left you barefoot and crying in the kitchen.

Her favorite was pop music, the songs that they played on the radio, songs that got under her skin and made her and her mother jump up and dance, laughing as they bumped into furniture.

Holly had dreamed about being a student at Haverty. Wondered what it would be like to walk out on that stage and belt out a song. But Haverty wasn't for regular people like her and her mom and their friends were. Haverty was filled with the best and brightest students from all over the country—students whose parents had the big bucks to afford it.

Holly and Wanda had little bucks.

Wanda Lovell was the best seamstress in the county. She ran her own business, Wanda's Sew & Sew Shoppe, out of their home in Biscay. She had a new Singer sewing machine that she'd gotten on sale at Wal-Mart last year, but she often preferred to stitch by hand. No one could tell the difference between her handi-work and machine sewing.

Wanda made all the dresses she wore, and

all the dresses, blouses, slacks, and shorts Holly wore. Wanda even did reweaving and could make holes invisible. Business was good, and although she'd never get on the *Fortune* 500 list of moneymakers, she earned enough money for her and Holly to live on. They just had to pinch pennies. And sometimes nickels and dimes too.

The first performer on tonight's *Haverty Talent Hour* was a skinny boy in khakis and a white turtleneck who looked to be around Holly's age. He introduced himself, then sat down at the piano and began to play Beethoven's *Moonlight* Sonata, a classical piece that Holly thought she'd heard in a detergent commercial.

"He's very good," her mom said, shaking her head in admiration.

"He's okay," Holly admitted. She'd been hoping the show would get off to a more exciting start. She imagined the boy turning to the crowd and breaking into a heavy metal number, startling the audience. Now *that* would be exciting.

Dusk was just beginning to fall, and Wanda had turned on the small fake Tiffany lamp, washing the living room in pink light. Holly studied her mom for a moment. She was so pretty, with her curly brown hair that just grazed her shoulder blades, and her nice warm almond-shaped eyes. *If it weren't for the birthmark, she'd be drop-dead gorgeous, even for a mom,* Holly thought, then hated herself for being so critical.

But it was true. Her mother's birthmark made calling Wanda Lovell a beauty queen impossible.

About two inches wide, the red mark stretched down one side of Wanda's round face, from her thinly plucked eyebrow to the bottom of her chin. Its crimson was a striking contrast to Wanda's lightly tanned skin.

Holly knew that some people looked at Wanda and immediately looked away because they didn't want to be caught staring. Their uneasiness was as pronounced as Wanda's birthmark. Most people in Biscay knew each other, though. Wanda's birthmark wasn't big news. It was just part of Wanda Lovell.

Holly and Wanda were closer than any other mothers and daughters Holly knew. There wasn't anything she couldn't tell her mom—she could even ask her about sex. Not that she'd done anything that she had to worry about spilling. Wanda still loved telling the story of Holly's first grade school crush. Holly had stood on a stool and puckered, waiting for little Tucker Ritchie to kiss her. After she'd counted out loud to three and felt nothing, she'd opened her eyes in time to see Tucker running away. She'd asked Wanda what had gone wrong.

"Next time count faster and stop at one," her mom had advised sagely.

After that, Holly realized that when it came to romance, Mom really did know best.

A rustle at the back door startled Holly from her thoughts. It was a second before she recognized the familiar footsteps.

"Did we miss anything yet?" Juanita Weaver and Ruby Simmons bustled in, putting their overstuffed pocketbooks on the kitchen table and giving Wanda and Holly hugs before taking their regular seats in the twin knobbed rocking chairs.

Juanita and Ruby were really Wanda's friends, but somehow they'd become Holly's too.

"Not yet," Holly said, wondering as she always did how Juanita managed to tease her black hair so high it scraped the ceiling.

"I'm sorry we're late—someone dropped by the house to pick up another one of Fifi's pups. We've found homes for almost all of the babies." Fifi was Juanita's dainty toy poodle, the most pampered pooch in all the South. She'd had puppies two months ago, and Juanita had been busy trying to match them all up with good people.

Juanita's trademark hairdo looked a bit wilted today, but her shimmery pink lipstick and starched flowered dress more than made up for it. She ran a beauty shop in her basement and was responsible for the recent wave of beehives and perky flips that were showing up on Biscay's Main Street.

Holly didn't trust her thick honey-blond hair to anyone else's red-manicured hands. But Holly would never get a beehive. Luckily, Juanita knew that.

"Whoo! He sure can tickle those ivories,"

Juanita said, her own fingers tapping on the rocking chair's armrest.

Ruby put a platter of pecan tarts on the coffee table, her rosy cheeks dimpling. "Just a little something to nibble on, ladies." She winked at Holly, who licked her lips appreciatively.

"I was hoping you'd make them," Holly said before taking a bite. Ruby's pecan tarts were a favorite in the Lovell house.

As was Ruby's devil's food cake. Her warm apple strudel. Her sky-high lemon meringue pie.

Ruby's anything.

As the boy continued to play, Wanda hopped to her feet and headed for the kitchen. "Let me get a pot of coffee brewing."

Wanda's kind heart and Holly's singing made their home a popular spot for friends to visit.

"I heard about a book that describes you," one of the neighbors once told Wanda. It was called *If You've Got a Lemon, Make Lemonade*.

"That book wasn't about me," Wanda had said. "Who can afford lemons? A book about me would be titled *If You've Got Ketchup and Water, Make Tomato Soup*."

Most teenagers would probably find it boring to hang out with a bunch of women on Friday night, but Holly didn't. Well, sure, she wouldn't mind being with Tyler, but when she'd explained to him that Friday night had always been her night with her mom, he'd been totally cool with it. Fridays were their mother-daughter bonding time, Wanda liked to say. They laughed over the outlandish outfits some of the Haverty students wore, or shook their heads in amazement over the talent some of them had. But it was more than just watching the TV show.

It was spending time together. After all, they only had each other.

Holly's father had died years ago, when she

was just a baby. Her mom didn't like to talk much about it. In fact, she didn't even keep any pictures of him. Holly often wondered what he'd looked like, and if she took after him—did he gobble up caramel corn like she did? Did he laugh at the same kinds of jokes? Were his eyes the same ice-crystal blue as hers were?

There were so many questions. And never enough answers.

Never *any* answers.

"Oooh, look at her, girls," Ruby said, biting into a pecan tart as a girl in a shimmery lavender top and matching pants walked confidently up to the *Haverty Talent Hour* stage. The girl nodded to Frank Shepherd, the host, and bent her head toward the microphone. "My name is Melody Gates and tonight I'll be singing 'I Will Always Love You,'" she said confidently.

"I guess her parents knew she could sing when they named her," Wanda said with a smile as she returned with a tray holding steaming mugs of coffee.

Holly frowned. "Shhh, Mom! I want to hear her."

The girl's voice was clear and strong, and she sang with an assurance that must have taken many years to achieve. When it came to the really high parts of the song, though, Holly could hear that her voice didn't reach them.

Without even realizing she was doing it, Holly started mouthing the words to the song. She almost always knew the words. She'd go from mouthing to softly singing. And then, as the music swelled, Holly would start singing more loudly. And even more loudly.

Right now she was in the middle of hitting the last note, her clear soprano voice one octave higher than Melody Gates's. Music swept Holly up and carried her off to a place only she could reach . . . a place only music could take her. Tuning out the rest of the world was easy when music filled her head.

As the song came to a close, Juanita, Ruby, and Holly's mom burst into applause.

Holly's face turned as red as Ruby's name. "I wish you guys would tell me when I start doing that!" she said, completely mortified. She knew she could sing—and she loved doing it—but she never wanted to show off.

But the women would have none of that. "If you don't have a voice that beats out every one of those Haverty snoots, then I'm a monkey's uncle," Juanita declared.

Ruby nodded enthusiastically. "Holly, dear, you have just got to get yourself into that school. You'd blow them away with that sweet song of yours."

"Why, the moment they heard you, they'd change that show and we'd be sitting here watching *The Holly Lovell Hour*," Juanita added, squeezing Holly's hand with so much conviction that Holly almost believed it herself.

Holly stared down at her toes, as usual embarrassed by the praise of her singing. She wasn't sure why it embarrassed her—it happened often enough that she should have been accustomed to it. A natural soprano, she could shift into alto easily. When she sang with boys in her church choir, she even improvised bass lines. Miss Fogarty, Biscay Elementary's music teacher, had once told Wanda that Holly had a four-octave range.

Holly was eleven.

That was a long time ago. Holly was fourteen now. And she was smart enough to know what was what. And what was what was that she, Holly Faye Lovell, daughter of a widowed seamstress in one of the smallest towns to dot the Magnolia State of Mississippi, had no chance whatsoever of saying hello to Frank Shepherd on the stage of *The Haverty Talent Hour.*

She'd sing in her church choir. For her mom and her friends. And in the privacy of her own room, where she could close her eyes and imagine letting her voice fly.

The television image began to flutter again. "Shoot. I'll never get a lick closer to Haverty than right now," Holly tried to joke, bumping the set with her hip once more. "But that's okay," she said, trying to ignore the sad feeling that swelled up in her just as the music did when she thought about Haverty. "I wouldn't fit in with all those hoity-toits anyway, right?" She smiled over at her mom.

Wanda held her steaming coffee cup between her hands. "The sooner you get going, the farther ahead you'll get, you know."

Holly fought the urge to roll her eyes. Her mom was always coming up with little inspirational quotes to motivate her. Wanda never failed to tell Holly she could do anything she put her mind to.

"Then I better get going into the kitchen to get y'all some more joe," she said as the strains of an all-girl a cappella singing group sang out from the television. She knew that the high school had a music department where she could receive training for her natural talent. *That would be just fine,* she thought. And then she busied herself with measuring out the coffee, wondering just who she was really trying to convince.

June 18

Dear Diary,

I keep telling Ruby I'm going to gain a gazillion pounds with all those good things she brings over. But does she listen???

When Holly hit that high note tonight, I felt chill bumps all the way down my back. She wants so desperately to do something with her life, to make it out of Biscay. And I want to help her. But what can I do? I would give anything to help her realize her dream, anything at all. Maybe God will give me the answer. He's sure heard me pray enough about it lately!

Don't get me wrong—I know my life is filled with blessings. Having Holly has made my world brighter than I could have ever imagined. I guess it's just that after working hard your whole life, and doing the right thing, you like to think there's some reward out there for you, a light at the end of the tunnel.

But I can't complain. My life has been filled with plenty of little lights all along.

Better go. Marge Maslow's daughter's wedding is just a month away and I've got the whole bridal party's alterations still to do! A mother's work is never done.

Tonight my evening quote comes from the

cutest little photocopy Juanita had. Someone got it for her off of the Internet (darned if I understand how that works!).

"Yesterday is the past. Tomorrow is the future. Today is a gift—the present! We shouldn't waste it."

chapter two

"He is so fine," Annabel Parker said long-ingly, fanning herself with a discarded flyer for Biscay's annual countywide bake sale as she and Holly walked down the cracked sidewalk toward Norwood's Auto Body and Repair. Summer had barely started and already it was a scorcher. "I mean, I know Tyler belongs to you and all, and you know how I think you two are the cutest thing ever, but puh-leeze! The way he looks in those jeans should just be outlawed!"

Laughing at her friend, Holly squinted in the June afternoon sunlight, watching as the owner of the jeans in question, her boyfriend, Tyler Norwood, bent determinedly over the open hood of a maroon Camaro, a serious-looking wrench in his hand. She and Tyler had been going out for so long that she'd stopped noticing things the way Annabel did.

A flash of Tyler's berry-red T-shirt—and the broad, strong shoulders underneath—caught her attention.

Well, maybe she hadn't *completely* stopped.

She lifted her long blond hair from her neck, letting the warm summer breeze tickle her skin. People always said her hair, shiny and the color of sun-kissed butter, was her best fea-ture—people who hadn't heard her sing, that was. "So how are things going with you and Billy?" she asked, curious.

Annabel sighed, her fingers playing with the rickrack hem of her homemade halter. "Just how they always are. Nowhere. I swear, what do I have to do, put up one of those flashing signs like they have outside the Dairy Barn over in Pearl Creek that says 'Attention Billy Franklin! I, Annabel Josephine Parker, am available!'?"

"That might be a good start," Holly said, laughing at the thought.

Annabel swatted Holly's bare arm with the flyer. "Now, just because you and your sweet little self snagged the finest guy in all of Biscay, Mississippi—all of Mississippi, for that matter—is no reason to make fun of the rest of us poor lonely hearts."

Tyler is *the finest guy in all of Biscay,* Holly thought proudly, her heartbeat speeding up as they drew closer to him. Tyler's lean forearms were glistening with sweat, his thick dark hair damp on his forehead. Taut, tan skin with muscles developed through hard work—not some Soloflex machine at a fancy health club like on the television.

Tyler didn't run with Biscay's rowdy boys. He'd never stolen a hubcap; he'd never gasped while trying to inhale a cigarette and claimed it was fun. From all her mother had told Holly about character and being your own person, she had decided Tyler fit the bill. He was, her mother stressed, beautiful on the inside.

Not too hard on the eyes, either, Holly thought, flushing. Tyler was her first boyfriend. She'd done pretty darn good.

Now that school was out, Tyler spent almost every day helping his daddy fix up cars. He had a knack for fine-tuning carburetors and tooling around with mufflers and rebuilding engines. It was a known fact that if your car was acting cranky, a visit to Norwood's Auto Body was the remedy.

Not to mention that Norwood's was the *only* remedy—the next closest repair shop was twenty-five miles away.

"Hey," Holly said as the girls walked into the yard outside the shop, the smell of oil and gas assaulting their senses. An old blues song was playing on the shop's radio. "Need any help?"

Tyler laughed, leaning over to kiss her cheek. "I want to get this car running again, not send it back to the shop." He smiled at Annabel. "Hey, Bel."

Annabel's face did that nervous twitch it did whenever she was around a boy. "Hi, Tyler." Then she gave Holly a wave. "I've gotta run. I'm supposed to baby-sit Charlize while my mom works an extra shift at the Piggly Wiggly." Annabel made a face. "She's going through a door-slamming phase."

"Call me," Holly said as Annabel hurried off. She took a seat on one of the old wooden stools just inside the shop. "Anything new?"

Tyler shook his head. "Nah. Joe over there's been working on that old Caddy since last Tuesday," he said with a grin, jerking his head in the redheaded mechanic's direction.

"I heard that!" Joe called, waving an oily rag at them.

Tyler Norwood has to be one of the nicest, cutest guys on the planet, Holly decided, watching him work. Actually she'd already decided that a million times before, but it was confirmed every time she looked at his face.

Like most people in Biscay, Tyler hadn't had it very easy. His mother had died of a drug overdose when he was nine years old. He and his dad had been left to carry on. The job of raising Tyler had fallen squarely on Phil Norwood's shoulders.

Tyler's dad wasn't a bad guy, and no one

could say he hadn't done his best, but he wasn't Mr. Mom. There hadn't been many homemade chocolate chip cookies or kisses on bruised knees for Tyler. Now that he was older, he was learning to help his dad run the business. Holly guessed that the love of cars must run in Tyler's family's blood. He worshipped them almost as much as his father did.

Working on cars for Tyler was like breathing was for most people. He said he needed it to survive. And when you saw his expression after he'd gotten a Mustang to purr like a kitten—and took it for a quick, secret spin around the block—you believed him.

"I'm gonna take a break, Joe," Tyler called over his shoulder, wiping his greasy hands on his old jeans. He and Holly walked to the shady elm out back of the shop.

"So what have you and Bel been up to today?" Tyler asked, lacing his fingers with hers.

"Causing mayhem in the streets of Biscay?"

Holly laughed, loving how her hand felt in his. "You know what terrors we are. Bel pressed her face against the Laundromat window and almost gave old Miss Lawrence a heart attack. She spilled bleach all over her dress when she saw Bel's fish face."

Tyler shook his head. "You better watch out or you might make the weekly paper."

He bent down and grazed her lips with his. Holly could feel his breath on her face, and when they pulled away from each other there was a smile on his face.

"I like kissing you," Tyler said, touching her cheek.

Feeling shy, Holly leaned against him, his words—and his kiss—playing through her head like a movie. She had counted the days until freshman year ended, looking forward to the summer months, to the time when she and

Tyler could hang out with all their friends. Shoot hoops over at the playground, play Frisbee in the meadow, eat cotton candy at the county fair, spend hours talking about nothing down by the river, just the two of them, when he wasn't busy with his daddy.

Holly had always thought having a boyfriend would be some great huge deal. "Don't get me wrong," she told Annabel, who hung on her every word. "It's cool. But it's not like it's the answer to all your problems or anything. I still get zits and do homework and stuff." Still, things were different with her and Tyler than they were for the other couples she knew. There had never been any big scenes or fights, no angry breakups or teary reunions.

"That's so high school," Tyler would say, shaking his head at the latest mini-drama.

"We're in high school," Holly would remind him, giggling. Tyler was a year older than she was. Her mother hadn't been too crazy about that. But once she met him, well, shoot! Her mom loved him almost as much as Holly did, and Tyler felt the same way about Wanda. He'd spent hours sitting up with her, talking about school and friends and television shows as if she were his age instead of being Holly's mother. Sometimes Holly thought Tyler secretly wished her mother was *his*.

That was okay, though. Holly was willing to share, especially with Tyler. Her mom had an amazing way of connecting with people, and her upbeat attitude was contagious. Every time Holly thought of what had happened to Tyler's mom, she said a little prayer of thanks to God for her own.

And for Tyler. Holly wasn't sure she knew what love was, but she sure liked him a lot.

A whole lot. He knew her and she knew him and that was all that mattered.

That was what made being his girlfriend a pain in the butt sometimes. Because he knew her *too* well. Once he got something into his head, he wouldn't let up.

"You know, 'stead of spending all your time renting movies and chasing after Bel's little sister, you should put this summer to good use," Tyler said, his expression serious.

"I should, should I?" Holly leaned against the elm, the bark scratching her back. She wasn't sure she liked where this was going. "Think they'd hire me at Norwood's Auto Body? I'm a whiz at emission repairs."

Tyler touched her face, his fingers sandpaper rough. "I'm serious, Holly Faye. You've got to do something with your talent. You can sing better than anybody I know."

"You're a pretty keep-to-yourself kind of guy," Holly teased. "You don't know that many people."

He let out a groan. "Come on, Hol. Everyone here in Biscay knows what a great voice you have, but no one else does because you aren't doing anything with it."

Holly was surprised at the emotion that filled his voice. "What am I supposed to do? Panhandle on the street corner?" she asked a little snappishly.

"Apply to Haverty."

She was annoyed at the way he said it, as if it was such a no-brainer. Didn't he realize how pointless it was? "Did my mom put you up to this?" she asked wearily.

He held up his hands. "Not guilty."

She exhaled slowly. "You two spend so much time talking to each other that you're starting to sound alike. It's scary."

Tyler hooked his thumbs in the belt loops of Holly's jean shorts. "Dreaming doesn't get you squat, Holly. It's chasing them that does. I care about you, you know? I—I want what's best for you."

"I know that. Thanks."

It was no secret to Holly that Tyler wanted to see the world. Travel to faraway places like Africa and China. Go on safaris. Visit the Great Wall. Ride to the top of the Eiffel Tower. Eat pizza in Rome. Race on the Autobahn in Germany. She hadn't liked that last one much.

"Now, how are you going to go to those places?" Holly had asked him one night last spring as they were sitting out on her porch swing, their stomachs full of her mother's fried chicken and hush puppies. "Do y'all have a secret money tree growing in your yard instead of moss and kudzu?" she'd teased, curling up in his arms. "Can I be a part of your dream too? Give me a first-class ticket to Vienna, Austria." Austria was where her favorite movie of all time, *The Sound of Music*, took place. She knew all the songs by heart. In her dreams she was Maria, waltzing on the Alps, singing like a bird.

She'd thought Tyler had been building castles in the air, fantasizing about what could never be, the way she did with her music. Dreams were that—just dreams. But he had pulled away and had stared deep into her eyes, a stare that had made Holly's toes shiver in her sandals.

"I'm serious, Holly," he'd told her, his emerald-green eyes shining. "Right now I'm here helping my daddy and learning how to run this business. But one day I am going to go to those places. I am."

And although Tyler and his daddy hadn't a dime to their name, Holly had believed him. Because she believed *in* him.

So why was it so hard for her to accept that someone could believe in her?

"I could write to Haverty and see if they

could send you an application—" Tyler began hopefully, as he had several times before.

Holly shook her head so hard that her hair stung her face. Applications alone cost money, and tuition cost money, and room and board cost money, and . . . everything about Haverty cost money.

Granted, she had wonderful, fantastic musical dreams.

But she couldn't afford them. *Zip.* She put them on the back shelf of her mind and closed the door.

"Can we stop talking about Haverty?" she asked, burying her head in Tyler's T-shirt. Besides, even if she could afford it, it wasn't like they were going to accept her, little Holly Faye Lovell from Biscay, Mississippi, wearing a handmade dress and getting her hair cut at Juanita's Shear Magic Salon—was it?

Uh, no.

"I smell like a grease monkey," Tyler said apologetically, lightly wrapping his arms around her.

"I know," she mumbled through a mouthful of cloth, loving the safe, familiar scent. "That's my favorite animal.

Holly's voice was rocking through "Working on the Building," an old spiritual. Her church choir had a new director, and they'd been learning a lot of wonderful songs lately. She liked mixing up traditional hymns with spirituals and more modern tunes.

She and her mom usually came to the first service on Sundays. It was a contemporary service, which basically meant that they weren't sticklers for any one kind of music. It was always changing.

The church wasn't big, but there were

plenty of brilliant musicians in the congregation. They had a terrific pianist, as well as some great guitar and harmonica players and some wonderful singers. Holly was always flattered to be picked to sing solos among such incredible vocalists.

The congregation began to clap in rhythm to the song, and Holly's voice rose even higher, pushed by her excitement, as she sang with the choir. She took one syllable and bent it into four. When she finished, she felt flushed and proud. She smoothed her choir robe underneath her and took her seat along with the others. For a second, her gaze fell on Tyler. He gave her a wink.

Later she had a solo. "'Just a closer walk with thee,'" she sang, her voice clear as a nightingale's. "'Grant it, Jesus, is my plea. Daily walking close to thee, let it be, dear Lord, let it be.'"

"Holly, you rock!" said a little boy in a front pew.

Holly fought back a giggle as her solo came to an end.

Since Juanita and Ruby didn't have families of their own, it was typical for them to come over after church on Sunday for dinner. Today, for some reason, they were a little late.

"Maybe they stopped at the fruit market to pick up some strawberries," Holly told her mom. "They know how you love them."

Sure enough, the two friends had stopped to pick something up . . . but it wasn't a strawberry.

"What in the world?" Wanda exclaimed as a tiny bundle of fur came tumbling through the back door.

"Ruff!" A peach-colored canine moppet

looked up at Holly—and promptly rolled over on its back, its little legs kicking. Juanita and Ruby popped in next, sheepish smiles on their faces.

"You brought one of Fifi's puppies to visit!" Holly exclaimed, picking the puppy up and nuzzling it. The puppy's fur was so soft!

Wanda raised an eyebrow. "Are you sure a visit's all you had in mind, Juanita?"

Juanita avoided Wanda's inquiring eyes. "Well, now, I just had one puppy left, and I know that Holly Faye's always loved my Fifi, and I thought maybe that—"

Holly cast a hopeful glance at her mom. "Oh, could we, Mom?" Other than a guinea pig that had died when she was seven, she'd never had a pet. Her mom always said—

"They're a load of work." Wanda shook her head as if she was convincing herself. "We don't need a puppy. I'm sure there's plenty of people who'd take in that dog for you."

Juanita pursed her lipsticked lips. "Now, I knew you'd say that, Wanda Jo. But just because my Fifi is clipped like a little princess and eats off my china doesn't mean this puppy would have to be as well." She cocked a thin eyebrow. "Why don't you just see how this little puppy acts here today? If she passes the test, you get to keep her!"

"Look!" Holly giggled. The puppy had found its way into Wanda's scrap basket. A little piece of muslin perched on his fuzzy head. "Doesn't he look cute?" she said as he scampered over to sit atop their Sunday newspaper.

"Uh-oh," Juanita said, hustling over. "When puppies see newspapers they think of only one thing!"

"And that's exactly why we can't keep her," Wanda said firmly.

chapter three

Big moments could happen on the most regular of days in Biscay, Mississippi. Like July twenty-fourth, for example, a day Holly and Annabel spent doing each other's nails, visiting with Fifi and her still-without-a-home puppy at the Shear Magic Salon, going for a bike ride up the biggest hill this side of Natchez, and having a sack lunch with Tyler and Joe at the shop (bologna sandwiches, pears, potato chips, and fresh lemonade).

"I'm home, Mom," Holly called out that afternoon, just like she always did. It was a private joke between the two of them. Their house wasn't much bigger than a shoebox, so Holly wasn't exactly hard to miss.

Usually her mom yelled back from her sewing room over the whir of her sewing machine or the whish of her steam press. But today the house was silent. A weird feeling fluttered into Holly's stomach. She shook it off.

"Do you think your mom could shorten this dress I got on sale at Vivi's?" Annabel asked as she closed the back door, naming the one store in Biscay whose women's line didn't look like it had been designed in 1950. "I was thinking I could wear—"

Holly started. Wanda was sitting at the kitchen dinette, an empty iced tea glass beside her and the cordless phone clutched in her hand. The air conditioner was going full blast. Her face was pale.

"You're home," Wanda cried, jumping up so fast that she knocked her chair over. The phone clattered to the linoleum. "Oh, Holly Faye!"

"What? What's wrong?" Holly asked, her mouth growing dry. She glanced uneasily at Annabel. "Are Juanita and Ruby okay?" Her mind was racing. "Is it Uncle Jake? I know he's been having those chest pains—"

To her surprise, her mother started laughing. "Juanita and Ruby are fine, and Uncle Jake keeps having chest pains because he eats too much of your aunt Sal's spareribs and sauerkraut."

Holly stood there, watching in dismay as her mom's laughter turned to tears. But they looked like happy tears, if that made sense. The proverbial tears of joy.

"Tell me then," Holly blurted out, panicked. "What—"

"They want you! You, darling. I knew it. I knew it would happen one day! Dreams really do come true."

"They? You mean I got the baby-sitting job I called about from the paper?" Holly asked, confused. She wasn't old enough to get a real job, but she had hoped that—

Her mother took her gently by the shoulders. "No, Holly."

"Then—"

Wanda's almond-shaped eyes were shining with overflowing emotion. "The head of the Haverty School of Music phoned here earlier today. They would like you to audition for a spot in the fall semester."

Annabel gasped.

A whimper escaped Holly's throat, and she blinked back the tears that were threatening to spill down her face any second. "But I—I . . . me? Me? How—"

. . . .

"Yes, you." Her mother threw her arms around Holly and hugged what little breath she had left out of her. "In four days you have an audition. At Haverty."

"You are the sneakiest, most lowdown critter I ever laid eyes on."

"How about laying your lips on me instead, then?"

Holly laughed before swatting Tyler's arm, making him spill iced tea on the carpet and sending Juanita in a fizz to the kitchen to grab a sponge.

The Lovells' tiny house was bursting at the seams with all of their friends and neighbors, who had come over to congratulate Holly. News spread fast around Biscay—especially good news like the Lovells had received.

I have an audition at Haverty! Holly thought,

pinching herself to make sure it was really true.

"You can stop with the pinching," said Annabel, materializing at her elbow. "You go, girl!" Then she lowered her voice. "Billy Franklin is here. I. Am. Going. To Die. Now." She took a huge breath, then sidled off, fluffing her hair.

"I still can't believe you went ahead and made a tape of me singing, let alone sent it in to Haverty." Holly stared up at Tyler, trying to make him feel guilty. But it wasn't working. He just smiled down at her.

"Hey, somebody had to do it." He tickled her under her chin. "I knew they'd love you. Those fancy Haverty big shots were probably peeing in their pants when they heard you belt out 'Working on the Building.'"

After a lot of prodding, Tyler had confessed to taping Holly that day in church when she'd felt so free and good. He'd also managed to tape her singing when she thought she was alone—a

Broadway show tune, some Top 40 stuff, and a Barbra Streisand song Wanda liked.

The din of the party yielded to the sound of Wanda slapping the television and Frank Shepherd's booming voice. "Live, from the Haverty School of Music and the Performing Arts in Hattiesburg, Mississippi, it's *The Haverty Talent Hour*, a one-hour recital that features the best young musicians at the best school of music in the South. And now . . . on with the show!"

A hush fell on the party and a shiver ran through Holly. Was it only last week that she and her mom and Juanita and Ruby had sat around, laughing and admiring the students? Now she was going to have the chance to become one of them.

July 24

Dear Diary,

MY BABY IS GOING TO HAVERTY!!!!!!!!!!!!!!! Calm down, Wanda. I know she hasn't been accepted yet. But isn't this audition a mere formality? Is there any doubt on God's green earth that they'll be all over her like white on rice the moment my baby opens her mouth?

When I stop for a moment to reflect on the enormity of the situation, a fear creeps over me. A cold, wet fear that seeps in my bones and makes me quiver. Holly Faye's never been outside of Biscay. Haverty might only be a two-hour ride away, but it's an entire lifetime of difference. I can't fool myself that once she meets all those smart people, people with fancy names and lots of money and such, she's going to want to come back here and stay with her old mom, can I?

Stay calm, Wanda. My baby's got a good head on her shoulders. She's spent so much time with adults that she's more grown-up than I am sometimes.

Yet what if someone there tells her the truth? I don't want to think about it. I know it's up to me to be the one to do it, but after all these years, after all we've been through together, it would destroy her.

Chicken. What I really mean is, will it destroy us?

Tonight I'm afraid my evening quote isn't the most inspirational, Diary. But it's all I can do on such short notice.

"How ya gonna keep 'em down on the farm after they've seen Paree?" Or Haverty.

One more thing, Diary. I'm going to surprise Juanita and Holly (and myself!) and give that little poodle a good home. This house is going to be much too quiet with Holly gone. I think I'll name her Princess.

chapter four

"D on't tell me that car is for us." Holly let the curtains close, her fingers trembling. "That fancy black car is for us?" Her hands were getting that clammy feeling they did when she was nervous.

Wanda, with Princess by her side, peeked out. "They said that due to the short notice they'd send a car service, and it's Monday morning at seven, so I suppose that's the car and driver."

With only four days to prepare, Holly had raced around Biscay like the Tasmanian Devil. She'd gone back and forth on what to wear. Students dressed in everything from sequins to plaid skirts on *The Haverty Talent Hour,* but she and her mom had agreed such liberties were not to be taken with an audition, not to mention that her wardrobe didn't include anything like that. Her mom had made her a pretty flower-patterned sundress at the beginning of June, and she'd decided to go with that, along with a pair of white sandals. Her hair was pulled back in a low ponytail, and she was wearing a dusting of blush and mascara. A few dabs of her mom's White Shoulders didn't hurt either.

All in all, Holly felt very grown-up.

And scared out of her gourd.

"Do you have the tape?" she asked frantically as she grabbed the pastel cotton bag her mom had made her and the lightweight cotton sweater she was carrying with her in case of Alaskan air-conditioning. The school had said she'd need to sing along to a piano accompaniment. She'd chosen a popular ballad from a movie soundtrack, and her church pianist had been kind enough to tape her piano playing.

"It's in my bag, where it's been the past three times you asked me," Wanda said calmly, smoothing down her beige pants and flicking a piece of lint from her matching polyester shell, bought especially for this occasion. "Now, you stay right here," she told Princess, putting up the doggie gate. Princess looked puzzled—then busied herself with her squeaky toys. "I'll be back real soon."

Holly knew her mom wouldn't admit it, but she'd grown awfully fond of the natural little clown they called Princess.

"Here goes nothing, then," Holly said, leaning down to give Princess a good-bye kiss before throwing open the door. She found herself hoping that the driver was nice.

"Good morning," he said, nodding and opening the door. Holly felt like a character in a movie instead of her real self as she ducked her head and slid across the cool gray leather, making room for her mom. She wondered what Tyler was doing right now. He'd wanted to be there to see her off, but that would only have made her more nervous. She'd be back that night—she could tell him everything then.

Her fingers reached over and touched the thin band of gold that circled her left wrist. Last night Tyler had pulled a small box out of his backpack and had given it to Holly as they'd stood saying their good-byes on her front porch.

"It belonged to my mother," he'd said awkwardly, taking the bracelet out and slipping it on her trembling wrist.

Holly hadn't known what to say. Tyler never talked about his mom, just like she never talked about her daddy. So instead of talking, she'd just inhaled. Sharply. "Tyler. I—I—does your father know you're letting me wear this?"

"He knows I'm giving it to you." Tyler took her small hands in his big ones and squeezed. "Your mom and you have done a lot for me, Holly. I know I can't ever repay what you've given me, but I wanted to give you something." He had smiled a shy, crooked smile. "My daddy said my mom used to wear this when she was feeling happy. I hope some of that happiness rubs off."

She spun the bracelet around on her wrist, wondering if it would, wishing Tyler's mom was still able to feel happy. . . .

"We're gonna have some story to tell tonight," her mom said, breaking into her thoughts. "I have a feeling our house is going to be party central again."

I just hope I have some good news to tell them, Holly thought, squeezing her eyes shut as the driver drove slowly over the bumpy gravel road that led to the interstate, wincing at every pebble that spattered against the sleek enamel. Would they tell her their decision right away? Or would she have to wait a few days? Probably the latter. *Unless they hate me,* she thought, slightly sick to her stomach. *Then they'll tell me thank you and good-bye right away.*

The morning sun peeked through the trees and into the car as it traveled down the highway. Holly dozed off; when she woke, she spotted the Hattiesburg city limits sign, which she'd always seen from the vantage point of a bus. From the car, closer to the ground, the streets seemed wider, the buildings taller. Hattiesburg looked like a city.

The Wal-Mart wasn't just a Wal-Mart but a Wal-Mart Super Store. Holly knew the Wal-Mart people only put Super Stores in towns that were special. They had obviously caught on, she decided, to the specialness of Hattiesburg, Mississippi.

The car passed the strip malls where she and her mother went twice a year in search of fabric and patterns. Today, though, everything looked different. Holly felt like the whole world should be in on her secret, cheering her on. How could anyone go about their business as if today were just another day?

It was the most important day of her life.

She took a deep breath as she went over in her head what would happen today. She was confident about her vocal skills. After all, she'd heard the school's best singers and was simply being honest with herself in believing that she could sing just as well, if not better.

But what about academics?

How would her education from Biscay

. . . .

Junior/Senior High measure up against Haverty?
She'd had some good teachers, but Haverty had
professors. From all over the country.

As if she could read her mind, Wanda
squeezed her hand. *At least I'll have her with me,*
Holly thought, trying to steady her nerves.

They were entering an older part of the city
now, a zone the driver said had been rebuilt
after the Civil War. "Course, Hattiesburg wasn't
damaged as much as Atlanta," he said.

"No, sir," Wanda said, clearing her throat.
Holly realized her mother was almost as nervous as she was.

HAVERTY SCHOOL OF MUSIC AND THE PERFORMING
ARTS, THREE MILES, said the sign at an intersec-
tion. An arrow pointed right.

Holly felt her underarms get sticky. *Did I
even remember to put on deodorant?* she thought
in a panic. *I'll be sweating buckets by the time I'm
through.*

She waited, almost weak with anticipation, as the driver turned the car onto a two-lane highway, the yellow center line so newly painted it glowed in the morning sun. There were fewer buildings and more trees along the route now. Haverty sat on the outskirts of Hattiesburg. She'd seen it, marked by a star, on a pamphlet about Hattiesburg attractions she'd picked up somewhere long ago.

"We're almost here," Wanda whispered, as if their destination were a big secret.

Holly nodded as the car turned into a hidden driveway and rolled between open wrought iron gates flanked by a gray stone wall.

A small black steel sign with chrome letters was posted in front of a row of small cedars. THE HAVERTY SCHOOL OF MUSIC AND THE PERFORMING ARTS, it read.

"The magnolias were transplanted as saplings from Georgia many years ago," the driver told them as they moved down a road flanked by the giant trees.

"How beautiful and fragrant they must be in the spring," Wanda said, her voice wistful.

The driver smiled in the rearview mirror. "Hopefully the little lady there will be a Haverty student so you can smell them for yourself."

Holly shot him a grateful smile. "I hope so too."

Beyond the trees, on either side of the driveway, was a lawn so thick that it looked like a carpet. The gently rolling grass spread as far as Holly could see. No weeds dared show their greedy little faces at Haverty.

"I think they manicure the lawn one blade at a time," Wanda murmured, awestruck.

Just ahead of them, up a slight incline, was a gigantic white building. The lane crested, and suddenly, there it was, looming against the sky. Towering white columns that glistened in the sunshine lined the stately porch, and deep flower beds filled with poppies and geraniums nestled around its base. Double doors at least ten feet tall opened into the lobby and were dwarfed by a second porch that peaked at least one story above them. It resembled an antebellum plantation. Holly was sure she'd never seen anything so beautiful in her life as the breathtaking building that housed the Haverty School of Music and the Performing Arts.

As Holly stepped out of the car, she felt like Rose when she first saw the *Titanic.* This beautiful building—and what it represented—was here for the taking, if only she could pull it off.

"Just go right on in there," the driver told them, indicating the double doors. "They'll be expecting you."

"Now, you'll be taking us back home, right?" Wanda asked, making sure in that motherly way she had.

He nodded. "They'll call me on my cell when you're through."

"On your cell," Wanda confirmed, as if cell phones and car services were a part of their everyday existence.

There weren't many people around—a few men doing landscaping work and a young woman toting a violin across the lawn.

Holly gripped her mom's hand and they started off. Holly's shoes sounded like clodhoppers as they walked up the steps and across the shiny wooden porch, and when they pushed open the double door, it creaked so loudly she was sure a SWAT team was going to swoop down and evict them.

No SWAT team. Just a welcome rush of air-conditioning.

Holly and Wanda stood uncertainly in a large rotunda with hallways shooting off in all directions. The walls beneath the high ceilings were lined with portraits of famous Haverty graduates. There were opera singers, members of symphony orchestras, popular music stars, and a few people she recognized from the Grammies.

The ceiling was painted with smiling cherubs and clouds and arrows. Around its base were flowery painted words: MUSIC IS WELL SAID TO BE THE SPEECH OF ANGELS.—THOMAS CARLYLE.

The marble floors were so highly polished that when Holly looked down she could see her face.

"It must take them hours to get the floor like this," Wanda said, running her finger along the mahogany chair rail.

"Don't do that," Holy blurted out. What if a security camera caught her? Would an alarm go off?

She took a deep breath, steadying herself. "Where should we go?" she asked, her whis-

. . . .

pered words echoing in the long, deserted hall.

Her mother pointed to the sign for Dr. Mc-Spadden's office.

"Is there a marching platoon here or is that noise us?" her mom tried to joke as their footsteps reverberated in the vast space. Holly tried to laugh, but all that came out was a squeak.

Dr. McSpadden's office was really two offices: the first, where his secretary sat, and the second, where he sat. Holly and her mom stepped into the first. His secretary, a blond woman in an expensive-looking suit, asked them to take seats in two of the armchairs. "I'll let Dr. McSpadden know you've arrived," she said, giving them a polite smile.

Holly managed to smile back.

The secretary went into Dr. McSpadden's office, and Holly and her mom sat, waiting, for twenty minutes. "Why did they have us come here at ten if they weren't ready?" she asked her mom, getting annoyed. "Isn't that kind of rude?" She'd expect this kind of thing at Biscay High, but not at Haverty.

Her mom shrugged. "I'm sure these people have many visitors to talk to. We'll be in soon."

The secretary's office looked like something from a TV show. The furniture was heavy and imposing, and shelves of books stretched from floor to ceiling. A ladder attached to a track let people reach books on the top shelf. Holly wondered who had time to read all of them.

Maybe people like her who were kept waiting for their appointments.

"Dr. McSpadden will see you now," the secretary said, reentering the room and motioning for them to go into the next office.

The president of Haverty stood behind a smooth cherry-wood desk. Framed diplomas hung on the paneled office walls, and leaded-glass windows looked out onto the rolling lawn. For some reason, Holly half expected Frank Shepherd, the host of *The Haverty Talent Hour,* to appear. Dr. McSpadden was much smaller than she'd expected. His head was bald, and he wore a gray suit with a navy bow tie.

Just because he was small didn't mean he couldn't be intimidating—think Napoleon— but Holly could tell by his warm blue eyes that he had a good heart.

"Welcome to Haverty! Hello, Holly, Mrs. Lovell. How was your trip?" Dr. McSpadden asked, shaking her hand and then her mom's.

"Fine, thank you," Holly said, fidgeting on her feet. *Okay, one question down and a million to go.*

"The car ride was lovely," Wanda told him. "We appreciated it so much." For a moment Holly thought she noticed Dr. McSpadden's eyes zero in on her mom's birthmark. But he acted like nothing at all was wrong.

. . . .

"So, what do you know about Haverty, Holly?" he asked, motioning for them to sit down as he did.

"I know I'd like to go here," Holly said truthfully. Her mom laughed nervously.

Luckily, Dr. McSpadden smiled. "I can understand why. We have over one hundred highly regarded performers, composers, conductors, scholars, and educators who make up the Haverty faculty." He leaned across his desk. "We have an instructor who won the Pulitzer Prize. Grammy Award winners come to lecture. Our halls are filled with published authors, recording artists, ASCAP award recipients, and acclaimed musicians who have performed in the world's greatest concert halls."

"Wow," Holly said, taking a deep breath. She'd known Haverty was an amazing school, but somehow she hadn't imagined all that talent being housed in one place.

It made her feel kind of queasy.

"Holly, let me be frank. It's very late in the admission procedure here at Haverty. Most of our high school students begin here during their freshman year, and our admittance decisions are usually wrapped up by April."

"It's July now," she blurted out nervously.

The president smiled. "That's right. But we've had a few slots open unexpectedly in the sophomore class—one student transferred, and another decided that Haverty was not for her. So when we received your tape, we were sufficiently impressed to call you in for an interview, even though it is summer and out of order with our regular proceedings."

He turned to Wanda. "If you'd like a cup of coffee or tea, Mary Anne would be happy to get it for you. I'll be escorting Holly in to see the scholarship committee, and parents are not allowed."

Before Holly could tell him that there was no way humanly possible that she could carry on without her mom, Wanda nodded as if she'd been expecting this. "I *would* like some tea. Thank you." She reached into her purse and handed Holly the tape. "Good luck, honeybun," she whispered.

Swallowing her fear, Holly followed Dr. Mc-Spadden into a third adjoining room. Three men and two women sat along one side of a long table, each with a pen and notepad in front of him or her, along with a name card. Each of them gave Holly a small, polite smile.

She gave one back.

Dr. McSpadden took a seat at the head of the table and introduced the committee. They were all professors of some sort or another, in voice, drama, percussion . . . Holly was a bit dazed by the credentials. She sat opposite them, and the interview began.

Holly had never answered so many questions in her life. And they weren't all about music or school, as she'd expected. The committee wanted to know what life was like in Biscay. About her family. Her friends.

"Who would you say are your biggest influences?" asked Mr. Felton, the youngest member of the committee.

"My mom," Holly said without blinking an eye.

Everyone smiled. "I meant musically," Mr. Felton explained kindly.

Holly flushed. *Duh.* "Well, I love Whitney Houston and Celine Dion and Mariah Carey," she said. "But I really don't know how much they've influenced me. I just open my mouth and sing what's in my heart."

"Can you tell us why you've never learned to play a musical instrument?" asked Ms. Gonzalez, her brown eyes compassionate.

"We couldn't afford lessons." It was kind of embarrassing to have to say that, but it was the truth. The committee members didn't act like anything she said was wrong . . . but they didn't act like anything she said was brilliant either.

"Have you considered a career as a music teacher?" asked Mrs. Barnes, cocking an eyebrow. She had a British accent.

"No," Holly said, the performer in her speaking a bit too fast. "Not that I wouldn't maybe like it," she said, backtracking. "It's just, well . . . I'm only fourteen. That seems a long ways away." Maybe, if a singing career didn't work out, she *could* teach.

Her mind was a bowl of mush by the time the question-and-answer session was over.

"We'll have a quick refreshment break, and then you'll move on to the written part of the admission process," Mr. Felton told her.

Holly nibbled on an overripe cantaloupe wedge and drank some bubbly bottled water. *I wonder what Mom is doing now?* she thought, trying to peek back into the office. She hadn't expected they'd be there so long.

After a few minutes, the break was over and an inch-thick exam book was set before Holly. Dr. McSpadden said she'd have two hours to complete the multiple-choice questions and the essay portion.

Now she was alone at the table. She could hear the lead in her pencil pressing against the cover of the test book. She could hear herself breathe. Heavily.

She stared blankly at the test book before mustering the courage to open it. *It's now or never, girl,* she told herself firmly.

The multiple-choice test was easier than Holly had expected. It was basic mathematics, English, and U.S. history. The essay parts were the hardest; most of them seemed to involve weighing a current event against a historical one. *The Dust Bowl ... Vietnam ... the Gulf War ...*

Her eyes scanned the questions. Then she looked at the clock. She both heard and felt herself gulp. Less than thirty-five minutes remained, and she was barely halfway through the test book.

She began to write faster than she could think. The writing looked like scribbles, and she knew it. *There's no time to erase*, she thought as she started rubbing the end of her pencil on the paper and then thought better of it. Just like when she sang a new song for the first time, she'd go with her instinct.

Her hand was cramped and she felt very tired when Dr. McSpadden came in to tell her the time was up and collected her test book. She was allowed a bathroom break and then was asked to report back to the committee.

"All right, then," said Mr. Felton. He pulled the cover off a piano tucked into the back of the long room. "Sarah will be your accompanist." He nodded to a college-age girl with bobbed brown hair and braces. She smiled at Holly.

"I'm not sure I understand," Holly began uncomfortably, still reeling from the written exam. She pulled the cassette tape from her bag. "I brought my own music. I thought that was what I was supposed to do. You told me I needed to sing along to a piano accompaniment."

Mr. Felton smiled, nodding at Sarah. "And you will. But live. Not on tape. And we'll choose the music."

Holly felt like she did when she rode the Ferris wheel at the county fair. Sick enough to . . . well, to be very sick. She'd never sung a song she didn't know with a pianist she'd never met.

She had sung to the piano and organ in

church, but at home she always used a tape. Her skin chilled as sheet music was placed on a stand for Sarah.

The pianist would play, and Holly would sight-read the music and sing, she was told. She'd hold a microphone that was connected to a tape recorder. After she had sung several selections, each would be played back, and she'd sing along with her own voice.

"We want to see how well you can phrase and then duplicate your delivery," Ms. Gonzalez explained.

The pianist played an introduction to a Rodgers and Hammerstein song that Holly had never heard.

And she played the introduction again.

And again.

Holly couldn't get her lips moving. Having these strangers stare at her as she tried to sing along with Sarah's playing was impossible.

Get it together, she told herself as Sarah began again. She couldn't let herself down.

She couldn't let her mom down.

This time, she sang the song with what she hoped was perfect timing and tempo. There was a song by Paul Simon next, and others by twentieth-century classical composers. She sang them as if they were old friends.

Then the tapes were played back and the committee members leaned forward in their chairs to see if Holly could do it again.

She sang each song with the same phrasing and held each note for exactly the same amount of time while harmonizing. No one had directed her to do that. She did a verse in the tenor above the melody, the next in the alto below it.

Her harmony was respectful of the lead singer's voice, which, of course, was her own. She knew that what she was doing was called overdubbing in recording studios, or so she had read. She never once drowned herself out. Instead she used her skills to enhance what she'd recorded earlier.

Usually people clapped after Holly sang. There was no applause today. Not even a little "You go, girl!" The tape player was stopped, cued, and turned on again. For forty-five minutes, Holly sang, stopped, listened, and sang some more.

In the middle of one of her songs, Dr. Mc-Spadden stood up. "That will complete your written and performance application to the Haverty School of Music and the Performing Arts," he said. "You'll hear from the committee regarding whether you'll be accepted or not in five business days."

"Thank you," she said, fumbling for her bag and shoving the worthless cassette back inside. *I blew it,* she thought, hurrying from the room and from the sympathetic smiles of the committee members. Sarah had had to play that Rodgers and Hammerstein introduction a thousand times before Holly had been able to sing the song. Her voice had sounded tinny and weak, not the strong, confident voice that was so loud and free in her room back at Biscay. And if that hadn't been bad enough, she had been cut off in her last song.

They didn't even need to hear any more. That's how bad she obviously was.

Don't forget the written part, the pesky little voice in her head piped up. *You know you probably blew that too. There's no way you got that question about the Cuban Missile Crisis right!*

Her eyes filled with tears as she walked quickly down the hall, not caring that her sandals were clunking along the polished parquet floor with every step. She had wanted it so badly. If only she could have another chance. But it was too late.

And when she saw her mother, flipping through a cooking magazine in Dr. McSpadden's office, the tears spilled out and slid down wet, disappointed cheeks.

chapter five

Holly didn't even bother checking for a letter on Tuesday. When Wednesday came she made sure she spent the day listening to CDs with Annabel. On Thursday she and Tyler went bowling with a group of kids from their class. Friday she wouldn't even look at a mailbox. She did the weekly food shopping with Wanda and helped her scrub the kitchen floors till they gleamed almost as much as the floors at Haverty.

Haverty. Holly didn't think she'd ever be

able to watch *The Haverty Talent Hour* again. She'd come so close, *so close* to being one of them. And she'd screwed up.

Still, when an answer didn't come in the next few days, she was a little surprised. "Are you sure you understood them correctly?" Wanda kept asking.

Holly sighed, the misunderstanding of the piano accompaniment still fresh in her mind. "Yes, Mom. He said I'd know in five business days either way."

I guess I'm not even worth the postage, she decided, staring at her reflection in the bedroom mirror.

"Pass me that nice pink velveteen now, would you?" Connie Phelps asked from her place in the sewing circle. "I'm thinking how sweet that would look on the border."

Holly dutifully passed the fabric. Once a month her mother had a quilting bee at their house. A group of ten or so women met and worked together on the same quilt. The one they'd been working on for months—which was almost finished—was a flowerpot quilt. Sunflowers and daisies and tulips sprang up in bright calicos and soft yarn-dyed solids.

Juanita sighed. "One day I'm going to learn how to quilt. I am," she insisted amid the women's chuckles, chewing on some pecans.

"Too bad Ginny couldn't have made it over here today," Wanda said, smoothing down some gingham petals. "We're almost done with this, and it would be nice for her to see it."

Ruby clucked. "That Ginny Anderson is as dull as a straight stitch, Wanda Jo, and you know it!"

Holly wanted to learn too, although she didn't much feel like it now. More than two weeks had passed and she'd heard nothing from Haverty. They hadn't even had the decency to write and tell her she hadn't been accepted, and after Dr. McSpadden had said they'd let her know either way, that was extremely upsetting.

Her mom and Tyler and Annabel had all tried to cheer her up. Holly appreciated their efforts, but it was hard to smile when your dreams had just been cut to tiny bits. She'd wanted to hole up in her room this afternoon and play some old Patsy Cline records, but Wanda had pleaded with her to come out and be a part of the circle, and at last she'd agreed.

A sharp rap at the front door made them all jump. "Drat. Ginny must have heard you," Ruby said, a needle between her teeth.

"I'll get it," Holly said, surprised that her mom's friend had come to the front door. No one ever came there . . . except Federal Express delivery people.

Not that that had ever happened before— except at this very moment.

"Is there a Miss Holly Faye Lovell here?" the uniformed man asked. He carried a white box in his hands.

"That's me!" Holly said as her mom joined her.

The man held out a small portable computer screen and a light pen. "If you'd just sign here."

Warm summer air washed over Holly as she scribbled her name.

"I'm sorry you're getting this so late," the man apologized, glancing around at the curious faces.

Wanda frowned. "Late?"

He nodded. "When we had that bad rainstorm last week, I was having a hard time seeing, and I thought the address said Forty-five

Kendall Court instead of your address, Forty-five Kendall Crescent. I left the package at the wrong house and they just got around to re-porting it." He handed the package over to Holly. "So again, sorry, miss."

She was dizzy with anticipation as she car-ried the surprisingly light box back to the cen-ter of the circle.

All quilting had stopped. The women were hushed—several of them for the first time in their lives.

"It's from Haverty," Holly said, barely able to find the words. Then she stared blankly at the return address, speechless.

"Of course it is," Juanita said, her face elec-tric. "Aren't you going to open it?"

"You do it." Holly thrust the box at her. "I don't dare." Her hands were slick with sweat, and she thought for a moment she might pass out.

"I will then, Miss Holly." Juanita slit through

the tape with a long red nail and the box popped open. "What have we here?"

Someone let out a gasp as she pulled out . . . a pale yellow sweater with a loose thread in the back.

The sweater that Holly had worn to her audition.

Holly could feel the muscles in her face slide like raindrops on a window.

"They—they sent you your sweater," Wanda said faintly, taking the box and dropping back into her chair.

Holly's eyes had begun to blink faster than a jackrabbit. "I must have forgotten it at the interview."

No one said a word. "It was considerate of them to send it using a fancy overnight delivery service," tried Olive, a round, plump woman with glasses who always cut her finger when she sewed.

Juanita glared at her.

Then Wanda let out a little gasp. "Hey. Hey, wait just a minute. There's something else in this box!" She reached down and pulled out a crisp white envelope.

Holly gulped. Once again, a collective hush fell over the room. Olive covered her gaping mouth.

Not even knowing how she had come to stand beside her, Holly helped her mom open the envelope. Their hands were shaking. Her eyes landed on *Congratulations!*

She didn't need to read any more. Wanda did it for her.

"You've been accepted to Haverty as a sophomore for the fall term!" she announced, tears streaming down her face as she embraced her daughter. "On a full scholarship for room and board and tuition and books!"

The cry of happiness that escaped Holly's

lips was the only sound she could make before the hugs and kisses and more tears came.

I did it! I'm going to Haverty! Holly thought, punch-drunk with anticipation.

"We're going to have to redo this quilt," Ruby proclaimed, cupping Holly's giddy face in her hands. "Can't just have sunflowers and daisies and tulips now, sweet pea."

A wave of happiness flowed through Holly. "Why?"

"'Cause everything is coming up roses for us and our gal!"

chapter six

Time in Biscay, Mississippi, had never passed so fast as it did in the weeks after Holly Lovell received the Letter. For that's what everyone called it. "Did you hear about Holly Faye? She got the Letter," the women would say in church, whispering behind their bulletins.

"The Letter, the Letter, shoot, I wish *I* could get the Letter," complained the other teenagers as they skipped stones down at the creek and blasted CDs on their boom boxes.

"The Letter arrived by Federal Express, can you imagine that?" the old men who played their harmonicas outside the pharmacy would tell anyone who listened.

Everyone in town was excited for Holly, no one more than her mom. They had until September fifth, when orientation for new students would be held; classes would begin the next day.

Wanda called up all her clients. "I'm afraid I'm going to be a little late delivering that suit now," she'd say. "I've got to get my daughter ready for Haverty!"

Holly sat on the floor in her room, her tiny wardrobe spread out around her. These clothes were fine for going to Biscay High, for sitting down by the river or going to the bowling alley. How would they hold up at Haverty? She was sure the girls there were going to have all sorts of fancy clothes, clothes she couldn't even come close to buying.

Then Holly shook her head. Why was she worrying about what she was going to wear, for Pete's sake? She had just been accepted into one of the country's most prestigious music schools because she could sing. Not because of her long blond hair or her handmade clothes. If the people there didn't like what she looked like, then phooey on them.

A minute later, though, she was despairing once more.

What am I going to wear?

Her mom eyed the mini-hurricane in Holly's room. "What's the verdict?" she asked.

Holly held up a few sundresses, some pants, and several shirts. "It's not looking too good, Mom," she said tersely. "I'm going to need way more than this. I've grown at least an inch since last year. None of my fall stuff fits." *Not to mention I'm going to look like the world's biggest hillbilly*, she thought nervously. She didn't even know what was in style. If the secondhand thrift shop look was popular, she'd be all set.

"I can make you two more dark skirts and a half dozen blouses if I sew every day," Wanda said, giving a blouse a critical once-over. "Might have to send some of the clothes after the start of school, but by November your wardrobe should be complete." She smiled. "What do you say you and me go on a shopping spree for some new material? A nice nubby tweed would make for a real cute skirt."

"Sure, Mom." Holly knew her mom was doing her best, but if only she could afford to take the bus to Hattiesburg and go on a real shopping spree . . . buy clothes with tags in them that said *Gap* or *Old Navy*, not *Made Especially for You by Wanda*. She'd never, ever say that, though. That would be some major disrespect, and Holly totally respected her mom.

"Mom, you'll be working almost day and night to get me ready for school," Holly said, guilt washing over her.

"Only for a few days," her mom said. "You've been waiting a lifetime to go to Haverty. My preparation will be short compared with yours."

Wanda sewed from midmorning until she broke for lunch. She ended up doing *some* work for clients; if she didn't, she'd never catch up.

Holly wished she could have earned money herself. No one had called her to baby-sit, though, and with only a few weeks left, it wasn't worth it to try and drum up business. Juanita let her help out in the beauty shop and she was able to save some money, but it wasn't much.

The night before Holly was to leave for Haverty, she and Wanda surveyed her belongings.

Her newly sewn skirts were neatly folded in her suitcase alongside her blouses and three new sweaters—one knit by Ruby, one knit by her mother, and a baby pink one they'd found at Vivi's for twenty-five percent off. Her toiletries were in plastic bags, and her pillow and bed linens and room decorations were in a cardboard box. Haverty would provide all her books and school supplies, and as she was on the meal plan, there was no need to worry about hot plates or dishes.

"I guess I'm really going," Holly said, leaning into her mom's embrace.

"I guess you are."

A group of neighbors gathered before sunrise to help Wanda and Holly load their dented Chevrolet. Annabel had said her good-byes on the phone—she said she'd never stop crying if she had to do it in person.

"Why couldn't you have found us a Corvette to ride in?" Holly asked Tyler as she hugged him good-bye. Her heart was hammering in her chest and she was afraid she was going to burst into tears before she even got in the car.

"I'm saving it to come and visit you," he whispered, kissing her on the forehead.

A lump in her throat the size of Texas had formed. She hadn't imagined that all of these people would come to help her and see her off . . . that this many people cared.

It hit her that she was going to miss them something awful.

"Hey, it's not like you're going to New York City or anything," Tyler said, trying to catch her in a smile. "You're only going to be a few hours away."

Holly sniffled. "I know that." It was just that if they could all have seen Haverty with their own eyes, like she had, they'd have known that going there was like going to another world.

A world of polished floors and fancy titles and people without thick Southern accents.

In a silly way, it was *exactly* like going to New York City.

Ruby handed Holly a cake. "Devil's food," she squeaked out before hurrying away in tears.

Holly carefully set the cake, resting on a paper plate covered with aluminum foil, in the car's backseat. There were hugs. Kisses. Tears. More hugs. More tears.

"Bye, y'all," she called out the window as her mom pulled out of the driveway and headed for the interstate. "I'll miss y'all like crazy!"

Her friends were still waving good-bye and chasing after the car long after Holly had turned around in her seat to face the open highway.

They had pulled off the interstate and Holly

was straining her neck in search of the sign that pointed the way to Haverty. It was a little after eight-thirty in the morning. Was there any hope of getting there before the other students showed up?

The car stalled.

No. There was no hope.

Wanda turned the key in the ignition, and the engine ground and ground. It began to grind more slowly, but at last the ignition caught and the engine started.

"Whew!" Holly and her mom exchanged relieved glances.

"For a second I thought we were going to be hitching," her mom joked.

When they came to the hidden driveway, Wanda turned the car in. Holly sucked in her breath, wondering if the school was going to look as awesome as it had the last time.

The school suddenly came into view.

As did the Mercedes, BMWs, SUVs, Jaguars, and Lexuses that cluttered the driveway. Luxury cars were bumper to bumper. There was even a limousine in the line!

It was stop-and-go driving as Wanda eased her old car along the circular drive where students and their bags were being unloaded.

"Oh my," Wanda said, her brow creasing. "This is not good."

"Speak to me, Mom," Holly croaked, turning so no one could see her face.

"The car is moving too slowly now," Wanda explained, wringing her hands. "The gauge says it's getting too hot. I hope it doesn't overheat and stall out."

"You've got to be kidding," Holly said through clenched teeth. "Please, Mom. Don't let that happen in front of all these people."

The car inched forward, then stopped, as

one by one all the parents ahead of Wanda took their time unloading their children and saying good-bye.

After fifteen long, tense minutes, they finally rounded the curved driveway and stopped in front of the big doors. The car's engine was smoking as Wanda shifted into park.

Holly pulled her things from the backseat faster than a skycap hustling for a tip at a crowded airport. It seemed that everyone around her had fancy luggage with wheels and handles that pulled out and snapped back into place. There were duffel bags in bright colors and plastic crates filled with computers and stereo equipment.

Holly had her old patched-up suitcase and a trio of cardboard boxes stamped TOMATO SAUCE. 24 CANS PER CARTON. She yanked one box from the smoking car so rapidly that it knocked the cake onto the sidewalk.

. . . .

"Ruby's cake!" Wanda said, crestfallen.

"Forget it," Holly ordered, any loving feelings toward Ruby diminishing in her desire to avoid at all costs the embarrassment of cleaning up chocolate frosting in front of her potential classmates.

Suddenly the car quit idling. Its engine stalled. Smoke poured from under the hood.

"Oh, shiitake mushrooms!" Wanda cried in a voice that suddenly sounded like some caricature of a Southerner. "What do I do now?"

Someone behind them in the line of cars yelled, "Move that clunker out of the way!"

"I'll just raise the hood," Wanda said quickly, flipping up the latch. A couple of guys standing near the curb laughed as she began to cough.

"Mom!" Holly said through her teeth, wondering if she really could die on the spot. "Are you trying to totally humiliate me?"

"Can I help you?" A college-age guy wearing khakis and a Haverty T-shirt came out and pointed to Holly's boxes.

"Yes, *please*," Holly said, trying to hang on to what little dignity she had left. The guy picked up her boxes and set them on a dolly.

Holly picked up her suitcase and got ready to toss it on as well. A girl with leather pants and a skintight white T-shirt walked by carrying a small leather tote and a matching bag that looked almost big enough to carry a tube of lipstick. She arched a thin blond eyebrow in Holly's direction.

This was definitely not the way Holly wanted to make her entrance.

"I can do that, miss," the guy said, taking the suitcase from her hands. "I should have been out here sooner. Let me, it's my job."

She bit her lip as he adjusted her belong-

ings. Every second that passed left her—
and the smoking car—open to public viewing.

And mockery.

Wanda fanned the smoking engine, the
heat from the car making her birthmark even
redder and more conspicuous than usual.

Holly took a self-conscious look around her.
Did everybody think she and her mama were a
joke?

Chill, she ordered herself. The more she
overreacted, the bigger spectacle she'd create.

Wanda tapped her shoe on the cement.
"Maybe I can ask one of these other parents to—"

Holly blinked in the morning sunlight,
unable to focus on what her mother was
saying. Holly wanted nothing more than to
kiss Wanda good-bye and get her out of
there. The cake, the car, the smoke, the birthmark—it was suddenly too much to handle.
A nightmare. Sending Wanda back to

Biscay was the only way Holly was going to wake up.

"Didn't we pass a gas station on the way in?" she tried innocently, pushing her hair behind her ears.

Her mother glanced back over her shoulder. "I'm not sure, Holly Faye. And I'm not sure I'd make it there—"

"You would." Holly felt desperate. "If you have to, call Tyler's daddy and they can drive down from the repair shop and fix it right there on the spot."

"But don't you want me to come in? Help you get settled?"

"I'll be all right." Holly leaned over and planted a quick kiss on her mother's good cheek. "I—I'd better go." She jerked her head toward the school. "Don't want to miss the orientation meeting, right? See you at Thanksgiving."

Before Wanda could protest, Holly fled to the safety of the double doors.

"Bye!" her mom called out faintly, unable to mask the hurt in her voice.

But Holly was already inside the building.

Fourteen years of togetherness were over in a few embarrassed seconds.

"So this is my room," Holly said to herself, surveying the mostly empty space in front of her. The college-age guy had shown her to her room on the third floor of the King Dormitory and had put her belongings inside the doorway. There were two twin bed frames with mattresses, two dressers, two desks, two nightstands, and a large walk-in closet with a row of hangers. Everything looked new.

Holly touched the hangers, the noise of the plastic clicking together loud in her ears. She was glad that her roommate, whoever she was, had not arrived. She could stake out her territory first.

The air-conditioning hadn't been turned on, and she moved to flip the switch. It was underneath the large window, and she paused, staring down at the scene below. Cars were still parked bumper to bumper, and parents and students were unpacking. She watched as a girl in white shorts ran across the courtyard and hugged another girl.

"I hope I make some friends here like that," she said softly.

She wondered if her mom was still outside. She was almost afraid to look.

Sure enough, a man with slicked-back blond hair, wearing a navy blazer that probably cost more than the Lovells' house, was fumbling with something under her mom's raised hood while her mom stood by and looked flustered. Clearly, the man did not often work on automobiles.

Suddenly Wanda happened to glance upward, seeming to look directly into her daughter's eyes. The sunlight hit Wanda squarely in the face. Holly had never seen her birthmark look more conspicuous. From three stories up, it seemed to glow.

Couldn't she at least try covering it up with makeup? Holly thought despondently. It wasn't that she wasn't proud of her mom—she was, and she loved her more than anything.

It was just that stupid birthmark. When they weren't in Biscay it was like . . . like the most embarrassing thing she could think of.

Not sure whether or not her mom could see her through the glare of the sun, Holly held up her hand and gave a slight wave. Then, before Wanda had the chance to yell up at her or do something equally humiliating, she turned and started unpacking, making sure she didn't pay any attention to the giant hole in her heart.

Holly didn't think she'd ever hated herself as much as she did at that moment.

September 5

Today was the absolute worst day of my middle-aged life. I had made a mental list of the things I wanted to say to Holly Faye in our last moments to-gether . . . our last moments before Holly Faye began her new life. I know, I know, everyone keeps saying we're only a hundred and fifty miles apart. But a hundred and fifty miles or fifty thousand doesn't make any difference, does it?

Tonight's the first night that Holly Faye has not slept under my roof since I brought her home.

I should have told her today, Diary. I don't know what's wrong with me. I had the words on the tip of my tongue and then I lost them, vanished forever. Holly had that radio cranking in the car and it just didn't seem like the right time or place to say what needed to be said.

The scene at Haverty was horrible. The car overheated—and so did Holly and I. I know she was just embarrassed of our situation, but I've never heard her talk so harshly to me. And for the first time ever, I . . . I think she was embarrassed of <u>me.</u> She barely even pecked my cheek—and I won't be seeing her until Thanksgiving! It's my birthmark. Am I dreaming or did it seem especially bright today? Holly Faye had noticed it too.

Can I blame her?

I had to pull over to the side of the road twice on the way home because I was crying too hard to drive. Then I gathered my wits, blew my nose, and stopped at a doughnut shop for some coffee. Wouldn't you know that when I opened up and saw they had put cream in it (I always take my coffee black), I just lost it all over again? I was blubbering and boo-hooing like a six-week-old baby. "We're

. . . .

sorry, ma'am, we'll fix it right up for you, ma'am," the poor young thing behind the counter said, rushing off to get me another cup.

I thought today would be the happiest day in my life. Instead, I feel more alone than ever. I'm losing my little girl.

Perhaps I've already lost her.

Tonight my evening quote is from Ecclesiastes, chapter 3. "To every thing there is a season, and a time to every purpose under the heaven . . . A time to rend, and a time to sew; a time to keep silence, and a time to speak."

God, let me find the right time for what I need to do.

chapter seven

"There," Holly said, hanging up the last skirt and giving it a firm tug on the hanger. She brushed her hands on her shorts and surveyed her work. It had taken her all of ten minutes to put away her clothes. They didn't fill even a fourth of her side of the closet, and her socks and underwear barely took up one of the four drawers in her dresser. She decided to tackle her twin bed next, and began pulling out her

sheets and blankets. Somehow, seeing the familiar flowered linens made her lip quiver.

She was just making a perfect hospital corner when the door to her room burst open. A
tall girl with shoulder-length dark brown hair,
twinkling blue eyes, and glossy pink lips strug-
gled to wrestle a suitcase into the room with
one hand and brush her hair from her eyes
with the other. She was wearing a striped
three-quarter-length top and one of the short-
est pairs of shorts Holly had ever seen. Her
strappy leather sandals revealed a perfect pale
pink pedicure, and her fingernails matched.

Holly found herself glancing down at her
own flowered sundress and sensible flat sandals and wincing. For some dumb reason she'd
thought wearing the same outfit she'd worn to
her audition would be neat. Instead, she felt
like a summerized version of Laura Ingalls
Wilder without the bonnet.

"Hi," the glamour girl said, giving her a friendly wave as a guy pulled up a dolly loaded with suitcases. "I'm Lydia."

"Holly."

"Don't call me Lydia, though. My friends call me Ditz." She dropped her sleek metallic tote bag on the empty bed. "I hope we're going to be friends—I mean, since we're going to be roommates and all, it would be nice to be friends." Then she laughed. "That was a stupid thing to say. See why they call me Ditz?"

Holly relaxed a bit. Her new roommate didn't seem the stuck-up rich type.

"How long have you been here?" Ditz asked. She went on talking before Holly could respond. "You won't believe what happened," she said, flopping down on the second twin bed. "I mean, my parents and I were in line with about a million cars and some woman in this total lemon breaks down right in front of us. My dad was totally freaking. He was ready to call a tow truck on his cell phone." Ditz laughed. "You never know what you're going to get here, right? So where are you from?"

Holly's face had paled. "Um, Biscay," she managed to say.

Ditz scrunched up her perky nose. "Biscay? Is that in Alabama?"

"No, it's, uh, just a couple hours from here," Holly told her.

Ditz rolled her eyes. "Geography is not my strong point. I'm from Nashville, and—"

"Lydia! We've been looking all over for you." A tall woman wearing a beige pantsuit swept into the room. "I don't understand why they moved you down to this floor. The view was so much nicer on the sixth floor. I'll have to have a word with Dr. McSpadden about this."

"Mother," Lydia groaned. "Holly, I'd like you to meet my mother, Valerie Hale."

Mrs. Hale had that snooty, moneyed look that villains had in movies and a diamond ring the size of a fat blueberry. Holly wished she had some place to hide.

"Now, where is it you're from, Holly?" Mrs. Hale asked politely.

Ditz waved her hand. "She's from Mississippi, Mom."

Mrs. Hale glanced down at Holly's banged-up suitcase. "And what brings you to Haverty . . . ?"

"Voice, ma'am," Holly answered, thankful that her mom was long gone. To her relief, Mrs. Hale didn't seem very interested in making conversation. The woman glanced at her watch.

"Your father's going to be late for his golf date if we don't say our good-byes now, darling," she told Ditz.

Holly watched as Mrs. Hale grazed Ditz's shiny hair with her mauve lips. "We won't be home until next week, so call Magdalena if you need anything."

Ditz nodded. "Okay, Mother."

With a wave, Mrs. Hale was gone.

Ditz rolled her eyes. "Finally! I'm dying to get downstairs and see if James has arrived."

"Who's that?" Holly asked politely.

"A total hottie in the classical music section," Ditz said. "He plays the violin. I dated him at the end of last semester, and he came to see me in the Outer Banks twice during the summer."

"Can the girls go to the boys' floors?" Holly asked, surprised. Ditz was mildly shocked.

"Of course," she said with a laugh, "as long as the boy you visit keeps his door open and as long as you're not down there after ten." She winked. "Don't worry, I'll show you where we hide so Janet, the dorm mother, can't find us."

While Ditz was off in search of James, Holly

slowly began to unpack the rest of her boxes. Wondering how she could dispose of them once they were empty, she peeked into the hall. When she saw one of the college-age assistants, she asked if he would get rid of her cartons.

"Uh, sure. No problem," he said, picking them up.

Holly wondered if she was the first Haverty student to ever shuck empty baggage. She didn't really want to know.

By the time Ditz bounded back into the room, Holly had put the blanket and quilt on her bed and had her framed picture of her mom, Tyler, and herself at the church picnic up on her dresser.

"James isn't here yet, " Ditz said with a pout. "Hey, when my mom talked to Dr. McSpadden—they're old friends—he said this was your first semester, and that you were the youngest full-scholarship student ever at Haverty.

Congratulations!" She narrowed her eyes. "So how old are you, anyway?"

"Fourteen. I'll be fifteen in December."

"I'm fifteen . . . and believe me, I'm old enough to know how to break all the rules around here!"

Ditz's free spirit lifted Holly's. She seemed like a bit of an airhead, but so what? At least she was nice. Ditz wore a tennis bracelet that sparkled with what Holly was sure were diamonds. The stones looked especially shiny against her deep suntan.

"So who's that?" Ditz asked, pointing to the picture.

"That's my mom and my boyfriend, Tyler." Holly had made sure to pick a photo in which Wanda's birthmark was concealed.

"He's cute! Is he a musician?"

Holly giggled. "The only kind of music he makes is with a grease rag and a wrench. He's into fixing up cars," she added when she saw Ditz's blank expression.

"Hmmm. Sounds sexy."

Holly blushed. "I guess." She and Tyler hadn't done much beyond kissing and hand-holding. That seemed sexy enough for her. "I'll help you unpack," Holly said, trying to be helpful.

"Okay," Ditz said. "I loathe unpacking." She pointed to a blue Samsonite travel case. "I never unpack that. It's always stocked with all my makeup and hair gels and potions so it's ready to go whenever I am." She ran her fingers through her hair. "I probably should get started now, so if James gets here tonight we can hang out. I haven't seen the Corvette he got over the summer. My father promised I'd get a car the second I turn sixteen."

Ditz would have her own car? Holly was pretty sure it would be a nice one.

"It's gonna be so cool to date a guy with a

car! We can go wherever we want and not have to kiss up to the seniors."

Ditz popped the latch on the first gigantic suitcase, which she had hefted to the top of her bare mattress before Holly could help her. She glanced in the direction of Holly's things.

"Where's the rest of your stuff?" Ditz asked. "You didn't get Walter as your baggage helper, did you? He's so slow. He won't have the stuff up here before Christmas break. I'll go see if I can find him. . . . "

"These are my things," Holly said.

"Right, I know," Ditz said. "Now let's see if Walter has the rest."

"No, this is all I brought." Holly could feel a slight flush spreading over her cheeks.

"That's it?" Ditz finally said, her blue eyes big with surprise. "Did your limo drive off with your luggage or something?"

"No," Holly said. "My mom drove me up

here. We don't have a lot of money. I didn't know I was going to be accepted by Haverty until a few weeks ago, and my mom sewed practically nonstop to make the clothes I brought with me. She's a professional seamstress."

There. At least she'd gotten who she was out in the open. She was so proud of her mom, the "professional seamstress." *So why does calling her that make me sad?* she wondered.

Before Ditz could reply, there was a rap at the door and the room filled with giggling girls.

"Amber!" Ditz said, throwing her arms around a thin redhead. "Finley!" she cried, giving a petite raven-haired girl an air kiss. Holly watched as they kissed and hugged and screamed. After what seemed like forever, Ditz remembered her manners.

"This is Holly," Ditz said. "She's my new roomie." Haverty didn't let students choose their own roommates; it was all done via computer selection. Holly was sure that if Ditz had had the choice, she'd be living with Amber or Finley or Charlotte or any of the other pretty, extremely thin, popular-looking girls who had just invaded their room.

"Hi," the girls said in fake polite voices. Then they turned back to Ditz and began to chatter.

If there had been any doubt that Holly had committed some major fashion faux pas, it was erased now. These girls all looked like clones in their short shorts and casual, expensive shirts with designer tags in all the right places. Each of them had a great hairstyle, and they all looked like they'd had a personal makeup application courtesy of *Seventeen*.

Annabel would drop dead on the spot, Holly thought, almost giggling at the image of her shy friend.

Face it, your clothes are your clothes, Holly told herself, trying to look busy organizing her sock drawer. She'd never been truly jealous of anyone's belongings before, and she didn't like the way it made her feel. Amber and Finley and the rest had spent a lot to look inexpensive. Holly had spent very little money to look nice.

"Hey, Holly," Ditz said, startling her. "We're going over to the campus cafeteria for some of Lucille's awesome fruit smoothies—wanna join us? The raspberry is killer."

Holly appreciated being included, but she shook her head. "No, thanks." Her regular meals were already paid for, but she wasn't sure how snacks worked, and she thought she'd die for certain if she was told in front of these girls that fruit smoothies weren't included in her budget.

"Maybe another time, then," said Finley in

a sickly-sweet voice, her eyes flicking over Holly's belongings.

Holly immediately hated her.

The girls spilled out into the hallway and clustered in the hall, swirling in the kind of confused circles that go with happy re-unions and with trying to say too much too fast. Holly moved to close the door. Maybe people kept their doors open in the dorms, but she wasn't about to do it when she was by herself.

As excited people often do, the girls talked more loudly than they realized, and their voices carried back into Holly's room.

"What turnip truck did she fall off of, Ditz?" one voice asked. Holly hadn't been with them long enough to put voices with faces.

"Did you see her clothes? Can you say *table-cloth*?"

"Her mother made the clothes, guys." Holly

recognized Ditz's voice. Gone was the silly tone she'd heard earlier. "Her mother is a seamstress."

"Is that all she made?" asked another girl.

"She needs serious fashion counseling."

"I guess. So what?" Ditz said. "I've got enough clothes for the both of us, and did you see her? I mean, she has a great bod. Of course, her boobs aren't as big as mine, but . . ."

The girls' voices faded as they walked away, laughing together.

"What am I doing here?" Holly mumbled, shooting an evil glare at the clothes that hung in her closet. The clothes her mother had worked so hard to make.

Classes hadn't even started yet and Holly had already learned something. The students at Haverty had a lot of money.

Well, maybe there were other scholarship

students, but she didn't want to be in a poor girls' ghetto. Anyway, no one walked around with a sign that said SCHOLARSHIP STUDENT. So, lots of the students—probably most of the students—had money.

And she didn't.

chapter eight

After her first month at Haverty, Holly was finally beginning to feel like she belonged there. First off, the place was huge. The number of students represented on *The Haverty Talent Hour* was just a tiny, tiny fraction of the student body—not to mention that actually getting on the *Talent Hour* was apparently so hard, most students never made it.

She'd tell Juanita and Ruby when she went

back to Biscay in November. They'd be surprised.

Holly was enrolled in the Haverty young musicians' high school division, which had about eleven hundred students. Nearly a thousand students were enrolled in Haverty's collegiate division—about eight hundred undergraduates and two hundred graduate students.

The student-to-faculty ratio was eight to one, and students came from almost every state and even some other countries. Holly had sat next to a girl from France in the cafeteria, and she thought it was one of the most exciting things that ever happened to her. For the first few weeks, the professors hammered home how esteemed the school was. Haverty alumni were members of all leading American orchestras, as well as many highly regarded orchestras around the world, including the London Symphony Orchestra and the New Zealand Philharmonic.

Holly learned that the school was named after William Thorndike Haverty, a wealthy Mississippian whose daughter was a world-famous cellist. Holly found out which professors were the famous ones and how to operate the coin washing machines in the dormitory. She discovered the quickest way to get from the Haverty Theater to the library, and which lunch ladies gave the biggest helpings.

All in all, it was a very educational beginning.

Holly had full days and nights, attending classes, doing homework, and rehearsing for off-campus programs. In the morning, she had classes in English, math, and social studies; music instruction was after lunch. Ditz was a pianist and took classes in drama as well. She and Holly didn't cross paths much.

Holly had been chosen for the Haverty Young Voices Chorus, an ensemble in which

Haverty students of all ages performed choral masterworks from the nineteenth and twentieth centuries in collaboration with the Haverty Orchestra. And she'd been psyched to get involved with Songs for Everyone.

Songs for Everyone was an outreach program sponsored by Haverty. Everyone in the voice department was encouraged to join, and almost everyone did. Student ensembles went out and performed in the community—in Hattiesburg's public schools and nursing homes and hospitals. Places that could use a little hope and good cheer.

Holly loved it. And Songs for Everyone also put on shows for groups that gave money to the school. Next year there was talk of performing in New York! Holly couldn't wait.

Many of the programs closer to school were on Friday nights, and Holly and the other singers in Songs for Everyone rode a bus. She loved being around people who loved music as much as she did. The Songs for Everyone shows were really good. But the best shows, she'd decided, were the spontaneous singing and jam sessions on the bus. She wished the public could see those.

The nighttime shows meant that Holly often didn't get back to Haverty until the wee hours of Saturday morning. But no matter how late she arrived, Ditz was always out.

One Friday night there was talk of a rare Mississippi snowstorm. Their concert was canceled, and Holly found herself home in her dorm.

"Hey, you want to go out with me tonight?" Ditz asked. "Matt's throwing a party in the game room over in the Woodwinds. I'm kind of beat, but it might be fun."

James and his Corvette were history. Ditz had so many boyfriends Holly could barely keep track. "Are you sure it's still on? It's been pouring all day and they're talking snow." Snow in Mississippi was not to be trifled with.

Ditz peered out the window. "Ugh. I guess maybe I should call first."

"We could just stay here and hang out," Holly suggested. She felt like she hadn't really gotten to spend much one-on-one time with Ditz in the weeks they'd been living together. "Go get hot cocoa from the machine and watch some TV?"

Ditz grinned. "Deal, roomie. Let me first just call Amber and tell her I'm bailing."

Holly took out a sheet of flowered stationery and started a letter to her mom. She tried to write to her mom and Tyler once a week. All the other girls were e-mailing and calling, even long distance. Holly called every Sunday morning after the campus church service and usually spoke to her mom for ten

minutes or so. Since neither her mom nor
Tyler had a computer, e-mail was out.

Dear Mom,

*Just got your letter today—aren't I speedy???
This week's concert was canceled because of bad
weather so that's why* ☺. *I might end up watching
The Haverty Talent Hour!!! Isn't that funny to think
of me living here and watching it here?*

*You must have read my mind when you sent me
that poem about success. I was feeling real tired and
boy did that make me feel better. I*

Ditz was leaning over her shoulder. "What
do you have to write to your mom about every
week? I wouldn't have enough to say to mine in
a whole month!"

Holly shrugged. "Just regular stuff. What's
going on in school. What I'm doing. Things like
that."

"My mother only wants to hear from me when I've got an A or won the part in the latest production." Ditz tossed her cordless phone on her desk. "I'd never hear from my mom if she had to write, not unless she dictated the letter to her secretary. And calling Magdalena for anything is like trying to get water from a tree."

Holly felt bad that Ditz didn't seem to have a very good relationship with her mother. That seemed weird to her. Ditz talked about her mom like she was an intimidating, busy person who barely had time for her own daughter.

Wanda could never be that way.

From time to time, Holly thought of how poorly she'd treated her mother that day back in September. It was too late now to take anything back, and she thought that bringing it up in a letter now that the time had passed would only make her feel worse.

She decided it was better not to mention it.

"I don't suppose you'd want to slip some JD into that hot cocoa," Ditz said mischievously when Holly returned from the vending machine with the cups in her hand.

"Huh?"

Ditz groaned. "Jack Daniel's. And you call me Ditz?"

Holly laughed. "That sounds totally gross. No, thanks."

Ditz shrugged. "Okay. Well, then, I can't do it because then I'd be drinking alone and when that happens they say you're an alcoholic or something." She picked up the remote and turned the twenty-seven-inch color TV on as both girls lay down on the soft plush carpet in front of it. "Ooh, look. It's a Julia Roberts movie marathon. I love her."

Having a rich roommate used to designer digs was a good perk, Holly had soon realized.

Holly had found out that Ditz drank alcohol

one night when Ditz came home after hours, smelling like a smokestack and puking all over their bathroom floor. It wasn't pretty. Holly didn't think there was much use trying to talk to Ditz about stopping, so she didn't try. But it bothered her. A lot.

When people were grown-up, they could decide whether or not to drink, Holly believed. But when you were fifteen, and trying to succeed in one of the toughest schools for the performing arts in the country, getting loaded every weekend didn't seem to be the best game plan.

"Hey, I meant to ask you," Ditz said, rolling over onto her side. "Can I borrow that little flowered blouse you have? The one with the daisies on it?"

Holly blinked. "You want to borrow something of mine?" Ditz had insisted that Holly could borrow her clothes anytime she wanted without even asking. And she didn't just offer

Holly her clothes; she'd put about half of them in her roommate's closet. Holly had come in early from a recital one night and had found the clothes and a note.

"Pick out everything you'd like to be seen in and out of," Ditz had written. It had never occurred to Holly that she'd have anything Ditz would want to wear.

Turned out she didn't.

"I'm trying out for the part of Laura Wingfield in *The Glass Menagerie* and that's just the thing mousy little Laura would have worn," Ditz explained sincerely.

Holly tried not to laugh at the unintentional insult. "Oh. Sure. Help yourself."

"Thanks."

They watched as Julia Roberts tossed back her long hair and delivered a witty comment.

"Holly?"

Holly looked over at Ditz quizzically.

"Listen. I *am* a ditz. What I just said didn't come out quite right." Ditz chewed on her lip. "I know you were sensitive at first because your clothes are homemade. I've never had anything homemade, but I think it's cool that somebody cares enough about you to take the time to make your clothes. It's like you've got your own fashion designer."

Holly had never thought of it that way. "I guess I do."

"So what'd she say in today's installment from Biscay?" Ditz asked, propping herself up on her elbows. "Tell, tell, tell." To Holly's bemusement, Ditz had become fascinated with Wanda's stories of Biscay life.

"Princess is getting into all kinds of trouble. She's chewing on our furniture and tries to pull my mom's laundry off the clothesline." Holly smiled. "But Mom says she's been suckered in by that cute little face of hers!" Holly was glad her mom had someone to keep her company. "Oh, and Juanita gave Ethlyn Chall a perm and now Ethlyn's hair's frizzed out just like Juanita's poodle, Fifi—that's Princess's mama. Ethlyn is fifty years old and teaches English at the high school," Holly added by way of explanation, grinning.

Ditz laughed, her face lighting up. "I'd love to see that."

"Everyone is getting ready for the Biscay Holiday Craft Fair. People bake pies and make handmade Christmas ornaments and the farmers give the little kids hayrides." Holly felt a pang of longing for her hometown. "Tyler and I went together last year. It's loads of fun."

"I bet," Ditz said, her eyes dreamy with vicarious pleasure. "What else?"

Holly picked up the letter and scanned her mother's neat script. "Mmmm, not much else. She's doing a lot of alterations on winter clothes and that's always harder, as the material is thicker. And, oh! She says she got a wonderful new blue velour that she's going to make a hat and jacket for me out of."

"You're lucky," Ditz said, her expression wistful as she turned back to the movie.

"I don't know about that, now. I do have *you* as my roommate," Holly said, laughing as Ditz bopped her with one of her sham-covered pillows.

Holly tried to concentrate on the movie, but she couldn't stop thinking about Ditz. There were so many sides to her new roommate and friend.

The Ditz who hung on every word from Biscay as if it were the latest gossip from Hollywood.

The Ditz who had pills to help her sleep and usually couldn't sleep without them.

The Ditz who could whale on the piano

when she wanted to . . . and the Ditz who mostly played the piano because she had natural talent, but no burning desire.

And the saddest Ditz of all—the Ditz who cried. Sometimes, when the hour was late and the night was quiet, Holly awakened to Ditz's soft weeping, the kind that comes from someone trying to muffle their face in a pillow.

No matter how plumped up a pillow was with downy feathers, it was pretty hard to hide the sight and the sound of weeping.

Everyone had their own problems. Holly didn't want to pry. If Ditz wanted to talk to her about it, she would.

After her first month at Haverty, Holly was finally beginning to feel like she belonged there.

Ditz, on the other hand, as Holly was coming to realize, was searching for a different kind of belonging.

Belonging in her own life.

chapter nine

"**Y**ou are really beginning to learn the value of restraint," Natalie Edwards said, beaming as she put the sheet music away in the small performance studio. "Can't you ever do something wrong so I can actually teach you something?" she kidded, her hands on her hips.

Holly felt her face flush with pride at her vocal coach's praise. She adored young, pretty

Natalie, whose own voice was as clear and bright as any pop star's. Natalie's specialization at Haverty was Broadway and pop, and she'd been assigned to work with Holly on those areas of vocal training, along with sight-singing and audition preparation.

There was a lot more to a singing career than Holly had realized.

On the way back to her dorm, she bumped into Ditz, Amber, Matt, and a stocky guy with brown hair whom she vaguely recognized from the drama department. Holly's roommate was wearing black suede pants and a form-fitting white angora sweater—not exactly off to the library, Holly thought wryly.

"Matt's driving us downtown and we're going to the movies," Ditz said, her cheeks flushed in the crisp November air. "Then we're going to this hot blues club where he knows the bouncer so we'll all get in. Don't suppose you'd join us?" she coaxed, showing her puppy-dog eyes.

"Can't. I've got some vocal exercises to work through—not to mention a paper for English," Holly said, glad of the excuse. She wasn't a big fan of Amber's. "Don't you have piano juries coming up to practice for?"

"Oh, those." Ditz waved them off as if they were dandelion fuzz. "I don't need to practice. I'm actually better when I don't."

"I guess you'd know," Holly said softly as Ditz and her friends sailed off.

"I have missed you so much," Wanda said as Holly brushed her long blond hair in front of her dresser mirror. Princess lay snoring on the radiator cover. "It feels like forever since you were here for Thanksgiving."

"I miss you too, Mom." Thankfully, her

mom's Chevrolet had been in much better shape when her mom picked her up outside the main gate at Haverty earlier that afternoon. "I wish I could see you more, but the chorale group takes up almost all my time on the weekend." A smile rose to her lips. "Not that I wouldn't love to see you, but it really is fun singing with such great voices."

"Sometimes at night I'm sitting watching TV and I'll start to ask you if you know the answer to a question and then I'll say, 'Wait. Holly Faye's not here. She's off at Haverty.'" Wanda shook her head, chuckling. "Or I'll be back sewing and call for you to bring me some extra thread from my tin and then remember that I'm all alone." She sighed. "I hope *you're* not lonely down there, honey."

Holly shook her head. "Oh, no, Mom. It's great! Sure, at first I felt a little out of place because all the girls have such nice clothes and all,

but once you get to know them, they're okay."
She smiled. "Some of them, I should say."

"Is it—is it strange sleeping there?" Wanda
wanted to know.

"To be truthful, it feels kind of strange to be
back here." Holly looked around her old bedroom. There was no color television, no
stereo—just her small clock radio. Her bed
looked lonely with its quilt off at Haverty, and
her closet was pretty empty since most of her
clothes were at school too.

"Oh . . . that makes sense, I suppose."

Holly put the brush on her vanity and
dabbed some moisturizer under her eyes.

"You use that stuff now?" Wanda looked surprised. "You know, a little Vaseline will do—"

"Ditz gave me this."

Ditz was always buying expensive department store makeup, and she insisted Holly take
the little samples they gave out when you spent

twenty dollars or so. "I've got a whole bag full of things," she'd say. "Take some if you want."

Holly's mom frowned. "I know you said she liked it, but I'm still not sure you should call your roommate a name like Ditz, Holly Faye. It just doesn't sound very nice."

"She *asked* me to call her that, Mom. All of us do."

Wanda's eyes fell on Holly's open suitcase. "What's this?" She pulled out a soft rose-colored sweater. "This is real cashmere!"

Holly smiled. "Isn't it just the prettiest thing? Ditz gave it to me as an early birthday present. I can't wait to wear it to church tomorrow night!"

Her mother's hands fingered the soft material. "Well . . . well, you'll sure be a vision in this, that's for certain."

Holly carefully put the cap back on the bottle of moisturizer as her mom sat, silently watching.

Suddenly Wanda jumped up. "Honey, wait right here." She hurried out of the room and returned a few minutes later with a small gaily wrapped box. "These—these are another early birthday present for you."

Holly had presents for her mom too—a new box of stationery and some potpourri-filled sachets she had made herself for Christmas. The gifts were still in her suitcase. "Are you sure you want me to open this now?" she protested. "It's only the twenty-third!" Holly's fifteenth birthday was the next day, Christmas Eve.

Wanda nodded firmly. "I know what day it is, Holly Faye, but I can't wait any longer to see them on you."

Holly ripped open the paper. A white leather box lay inside. She opened the lid. "Oh, Mom," she breathed, lifting a strand of glistening pearls from a velveteen liner. "They're beautiful."

Wanda rocked back on Holly's bed, looking pleased as punch. "They'll look awfully nice with that cashmere sweater."

Holly had seen pearls like this on some of the wealthiest girls at Haverty. "How on earth did you afford them on what you make?"

Wanda looked like she was going to say something, but stopped. "Oh . . . well, business has picked up a lot lately, and when I saw these . . . these . . . on sale down at Gower's, I— I just had to get them."

Holly's smile faded a bit. "Thanks, Mom. I— I really love them." She reached over and gave her mom a hug, then laid the pearls back in their box.

"Come to the kitchen when you're finished and I'll reheat that apple pie," Wanda said, rising to answer the ringing phone.

"Okay."

Alone, Holly lifted the pearls and studied

them. At first she'd thought they were real. But when her mom told her where she'd bought them—at Gower's, the store that specialized in earrings for three dollars and handbags for ten, Holly realized they couldn't be.

I'll wear these while I'm home, but there's no way I can wear them back at Haverty, Holly thought resignedly, putting the box in her suitcase anyway. She didn't want her friends at school thinking she was trying to imitate the way they dressed, and she knew they'd be able to recognize a fake in an instant.

Too bad. They really are pretty.

"So tell us all about it. Are there cameras following you everywhere? Do the professors who have Grammies have them sitting on their desks? Have you seen anyone famous there? Is Frank Shepherd as handsome as he is on TV?"

. . . .

Holly couldn't stop laughing. She hadn't been able to get home for more than two days at Thanksgiving, as Songs for Everyone had scheduled several concerts over the holiday weekend. Now that it was Christmas, she had two weeks to spend back in Biscay, and Annabel wasn't wasting a minute pumping her for information.

"No to the first three, and I have no idea about the last," she said, taking another big bite of ham. Her mom had been making all her favorite foods while she was home, and tonight's menu of baked honey ham, scalloped potatoes, and green bean casserole had been too good to make for just the two of them. Annabel, Tyler, Juanita, and Ruby had been more than happy to join the feast.

"So when do you reckon you'll be on *The Haverty Talent Hour*?" Juanita asked, passing the potatoes. "I keep tuning in each week, but I know you'd surely let us hear if that was about to happen."

"Don't know what they're waiting for," added Ruby, shaking her head and simultaneously blotting her lips with her napkin. She slipped Princess a scrap of ham.

"Y'all are awfully nice to keep saying that, but performing on the show is an honor reserved for juniors and seniors," Holly explained. "Keep your fingers crossed for next year, though!"

Tyler smiled over at her. Holly thought he looked especially cute in the new flannel shirt Wanda had given him for Christmas. His hair curled over the collar and his chest looked broad and strong.

"Hey, you already broke one rule by being the youngest scholarship student ever at Haverty," he reminded her, his eyes twinkling. "Don't see why you can't break another."

Later, after everyone else had gone home,

Holly and Tyler sat side by side on the couch, an investigative news show flashing images on the television. But they weren't really watching.

"Yep," Tyler said, leaning back with his hands clasped behind his head of wavy brown hair. "Randy Jack is still giving all the poor teachers at Biscay High a daily dose of heartburn. And the food in the cafeteria still sucks."

"Except for the chicken tacos," they said together, laughing.

Holly had missed Tyler like crazy in the beginning. But somehow they'd gotten through it, getting by on letters and an occasional phone call. Next year Tyler would be old enough to drive, and he could come and visit her on her free weekends. He still ate Sunday dinner at Holly's house with his daddy. Juanita had whispered to her that she thought Phil Norwood was getting sweet on Holly's mom.

Her mom and Tyler's dad? Could it be true?

That was too weird to think about. Then Holly had laughed out loud. On second thought, it wouldn't be the *worst* thing to happen.

"You seem really happy," Tyler said now.

Holly met his eyes, serious for the first time that night. "I am. At first, it was like I wrote to you," she told him. "A lot of the girls seemed real snobby and I wasn't sure I was going to fit in. But my roommate, Ditz, is really nice, and the vocal program is just so amazing." She was quiet for a moment. "I guess I know how lucky I am to be there."

"Doesn't mean I don't miss you, though," Tyler said, putting his solid arm around Holly's shoulder. He pretended to look confused. "Now, I forget. How many more years do you have there?"

"Three," she said, laughing.

"Oh, well, see, I'd stop waiting for you after four. You just make the cutoff."

Holly giggled. She loved it that he said that. And she loved the feel of his arm around her even more.

She wouldn't trade Tyler Norwood for a million Haverty boys—even ones that drove Corvettes.

December 28

Dear Diary,

I don't know what was worse—giving Holly Faye those pearls the day before her birthday or not telling her the truth about them being real. When I heard her talking about her fancy friend and saw that gorgeous sweater she gave her, something came over me and I—I'm ashamed to say it—I felt like I had to compete with those Haverty people just to make sure she wouldn't replace me. That sweater must have cost two hundred dollars! I don't have much in the material way to offer her, but the pearls—the pearls surely cost more than I make in a year. But then, when she asked me where I got them,

I heard myself stammering and stuttering and making up some lie about Gower's.

A lie because I'm afraid to tell her the truth. The whole truth.

When am I going to get the courage? The year is almost up and I swore I'd do it on her birthday. Then Christmas. But then I realized that would ruin her holidays . . . so now when? When's the next date I can give myself and miss it? New Year's Eve? Juanita and Ruby are so angry with me. They keep telling me I must tell Holly Faye the truth before someone else does . . . and while I know they're right, I can't make my lips say the words that need to be said.

It's becoming more and more difficult to say anything with each day that passes. The ties that bind us as mother and daughter are already fraying, wearing away with her living in Hattiesburg. If I tell her the truth it's bound to destroy us completely.

156

Please Lord, help me.

Tonight I'm looking for inspiration from the words of Dr. Martin Luther King, Jr. "I believe that unarmed truth and unconditional love will have the final word in reality."

If only I could be so brave as that fine man was.

chapter ten

"No, Ms. Gonzalez, I haven't seen Dit—I mean Lydia today." Holly bit her lip as Ditz's manicured hand, sticking out from under her comforter, frantically motioned to her to continue.

It wasn't exactly a lie.

"I—I will, Ms. Gonzalez. Yes. Yes, I know how important it is to get on the right track now that it's January. Yes. Yes, I'll tell her. Good-bye." Holly clicked off the phone and yanked the comforter away from Ditz.

"Hey, it's freezing!" Ditz howled, scrambling to wrap herself in the blanket that had been under the comforter. Then she groaned. "Why do you have the blinds open? It's way bright in here."

"I have the blinds open because it's noon," Holly said curtly. "I forgot my English book and ran back to get it and here you are wasting the day." *Because you were out goofing around last night, just like you have been for the past month,* she added silently. "I'm not going to do your dirty work and put off your teachers. You've got to start going to class, Ditz. If you don't, they're going to call your parents and put you on probation." She yanked the blanket off Ditz for emphasis. "Maybe even kick you out!"

Lately Ditz had seemed more reckless than ever. Not only did she keep a bottle of peach

liquor stashed in their room, but she was con-
stantly cutting classes and sneaking out after
hours. Holly couldn't believe she hadn't been
caught yet. It tied her stomach in knots just
thinking about it.

Her roommate was playing with fire.

Ditz snorted, yanking the plug from the
phone base. "They wouldn't dare. My daddy
would have his attorneys on the phone so fast it
would make their heads spin. Besides," she
said, stuffing her pillow under her neck, "my
mom and Dr. McSpadden are tight. He would
never let them kick me out."

Maybe that's true, Holly thought as she re-
trieved her book from the shelf and quietly
closed the door.

She had a bad feeling that Ditz was about to
find out.

• • •

Tyler surprised Holly with two bus trips to Haverty that winter—he'd called and checked first to be sure she wasn't on the road. When Ditz and Tyler had met, Holly had felt a momentary pang—how could Tyler not fall for her beautiful, funny friend? But Tyler had only had eyes for her.

"Don't be surprised if you see me again real soon," Tyler had told her as they breathed cold evening air, waiting for the bus that would take him home. "I can't help it if I miss you so darn much."

Holly had blinked back tears as he bent to kiss her. Kissing Tyler always made her feel happy . . . except when they were kissing good-bye.

"Once you taste Brady's Bake Shop brownies, you'll know why I'm making such a big deal over them." Ditz rubbed her flat stomach in anticipation. Her hair was pulled up in a messy ponytail, and she was wearing a new mint-green trench coat with a pair of white Keds. "In fact, I might need to call my mom back and ask her to bring three tins instead of two."

"She's already carting half of Nashville down here with all the requests you've e-mailed Magdalena," Holly said, zipping up her jacket as they walked down the busy corridor of the main Haverty building. "Besides, you're too late. Your parents must have left already, right?" February's Parents' Weekend festivities would start the next day, and it was all Ditz had talked about for the past few weeks.

"Nope. They're flying out tomorrow morning," Ditz said, popping a piece of gum into her mouth.

Holly couldn't believe the kind of money

Ditz's family spent on things. Flying down to Mississippi for the weekend. She'd never even been in an airport, let alone on an airplane.

"I still don't understand why your mother couldn't get someone else to pitch in and help her finish all her work so she could come too." Ditz sighed. "I was really looking forward to meeting her. After all your letters, I feel like I know her."

Holly fiddled with her binder. "I wish she could have . . . there's always another time, though, right?" She knew her mom would have shown up with bells and whistles on.

If only Holly had *told* her about Parents' Weekend.

But having her mom show up in her old car with her birthmark sending out a strobe light from her face was not something Holly wanted to happen. She knew it was horrible, but that was how she felt. So she'd told everyone who cared that her mom was too busy with her work to come. Lots of kids had mothers who were too busy working or on business trips, so for many it was no big deal.

The truth was, she hadn't even mentioned it to Wanda.

Everyone had believed her lie. Holly hadn't realized how easy it was to fool people.

Or how bad it would make her feel.

"You'll just have to be with us, then," Ditz declared, linking her arm in Holly's. "I want to show my parents the new rehearsal hall, and maybe we'll take one of those campus tours run by those hunky guys in the jazz section. It'll all be new to them; they weren't able to come last year because my granny was real sick. Then there's the bonfire at night and the sing-along, and then we'll go out to dinner." Ditz's face grew animated. "Then we'll have brunch on Sunday before they leave."

"You haven't seen your parents in a long time, though," Holly said as they headed back to the dorm. "Maybe the three of you just want to do stuff alone." The realization that she could have been having fun with her own mom buzzed like a mosquito in her ear. She swatted the thought away.

"My parents won't care," Ditz said, a little less animated. A bit of the sparkle had left her eyes. "Besides, if your mom can't be here, you'll just have to share mine."

Was that a good thing? Holly wasn't sure.

"Isn't this great?" Ditz said merrily over the din of the crowd as she, her parents, and Holly sat jammed together on an outdoor bench. The bonfire raged high above them, its flames licking the inky black sky. A reggae band composed of Haverty students was playing Bob

Marley tunes, and a bunch of people were dancing.

Holly suspected this wasn't the kind of entertainment Peter and Valerie Hale of the Nashville Hales usually enjoyed.

Mrs. Hale brushed some invisible lint off her navy blazer. Her shoulder-length blond hair was streaked with honeyed highlights, and Holly thought she'd be quite pretty if she smiled. "I was hoping we'd run into Amber Jackson's parents. I haven't seen Polly and David since we crossed paths in Aruba in December."

Mr. Hale didn't even bother to force another smile before checking his watch for the fourth time. "Aren't we running a bit behind schedule?" He reminded Holly of one of those Wall Street men she'd seen in movies, with his fast way of talking and his expensive tailored clothes.

. . . .

"I don't think it'll be too much longer, Dad." Ditz wore a hopeful, eager expression. "It's just, well, I wanted you to see the spirit of Haverty. The camaraderie, the bonfires, the people." She waggled her eyebrows. "The cute guy from the piano department."

"The drain all my money is pouring down is more like it," Mr. Hale said. Holly wasn't sure if he was joking or not.

From the moment Mr. and Mrs. Hale's limousine had arrived at Haverty, they had complained. The buildings were too far apart. They couldn't hear the tour guide. The weather was damp and misty.

Even cheerful, peppy Ditz was beginning to droop a little. As for Holly, after walking all over campus, standing in line for a buffet lunch in the cafeteria with all the other students and their visiting parents, and helping her Songs for Everyone friends plan their part in an afternoon showcase of the many programs at Haverty, she had been looking forward to sitting.

All Mr. and Mrs. Hale appeared to be looking forward to was their flight home.

Mrs. Hale began coughing. "This smoke is irritating my contacts. And I am ice cold. I had no idea they would go through with a bonfire when the temperature is in the fifties!" She shuddered.

"How about I go get us some hot chocolate?" Holly said, glad of the excuse to bolt.

"That'd be nice, Holly. Thanks," Ditz said gratefully.

Mrs. Hale gave Holly a brief wave before answering her ringing cell phone.

Holly couldn't help noticing that ever since the Hales had arrived, Ditz had been jumping through hoops. After all the weeks of excited planning, Holly had been expecting to see the reunion of a happy family, the kind she'd watched on TV. Instead, these people seemed to be counting the minutes until they could leave.

She bought four hot chocolates from the vendor's cart and put them in one of the little cardboard carriers before heading back to the Hales. *If Mom was here, we'd be having such a good time*, she thought guiltily, knowing how much her mom would have loved the tour of the campus, and how proud she would have been to see Holly up onstage performing with her classmates. Wanda never would have complained about the cold or checked her watch. *Why does she have to have that stupid red birthmark? And our car is such an embarrassment.* Holly felt her own face turn red as she realized how mean-spirited she felt.

Mrs. Hale's nasal voice carried over the crowd as Holly approached. "Excuse me, but wasn't the idea to spend some time with

Lydia?" she was saying to Mr. Hale. "Who knew we'd have the little orphan scholarship girl tagging along too?"

Holly stopped short, hot chocolate sloshing out of one of the cups. *Little orphan scholarship girl? Is that what they think? But I have a mother.* It occurred to her that her mom could have taken the 6:30 A.M. bus instead of driving up if Holly had only thought of it.

Holly stared down at her worn penny loafers, little clumps of mud stuck to the toes. How could Mrs. Hale act nice to her face and then say something so awful? Yet Holly felt pretty sure that if it hadn't been for her, Ditz would have been having a completely miserable time instead of only a semi-miserable one, since her parents were so unpleasant.

It didn't matter if the Hales were phonies. Ditz was their daughter, and she wasn't anything like them.

She was Holly's one real Haverty friend.

Holding her head as high as she could, Holly walked back to the bench, balancing the hot chocolates carefully.

"Thank you so much," Mrs. Hale said, flashing a smile at her as she took a cup. Mr. Hale did the same.

"Oh, no, you spilled yours," Ditz said, noticing the half-empty container that Holly had quickly claimed as her own.

"That's okay," Holly said quietly. "I'm not that thirsty anyway."

"So I guess this is good-bye, then." Holly stood on the sidelines as Ditz smiled awkwardly at the Hales like they were two strangers instead of her parents.

Maybe they were.

They were standing outside the massive

brass-handled doors that led to the Haverty Theater. Students and parents streamed inside for the sing-along.

Not the Hales.

Mr. Hale had been called back to Nashville for an urgent meeting at the company he ran, and the Hales had had to cancel their plans to join in the evening's events in order to make their rescheduled flight.

I'm sure this is important and all, but how can they do this to Ditz? Holly wondered in disbelief as Mr. Hale signaled to their limousine driver and Mrs. Hale gave her daughter a showy hug. Ditz had been so psyched to have them there— and now they were leaving early.

"Keep up the good work, Lydia," Mr. Hale said, squeezing Ditz's thin shoulders. "No tears," he chided as Ditz's eyes started to water. "You go inside with your friends and have fun at your singathon."

"Remember, honey, the pageants always love girls who can play the piano," Mrs. Hale said, smoothing back Ditz's windblown hair.

"I know." Ditz sniffled. "Thanks for coming. I—I just wish you could have stayed longer, like we'd planned."

"Now, honey. Don't make us feel guilty!" Mrs. Hale turned a pitying gaze on Holly. "Some parents didn't even show up."

Holly swallowed. She wasn't sure what she could say to that. *My mom would never bail on me,* she thought. *If I gave her the opportunity in the first place, that is.*

Holly wished Mr. and Mrs. Hale a good trip back to Nashville, then moved inside the theater so Ditz could say her final good-byes with her parents in private. When Ditz stepped inside the theater a few seconds later, her eyes were rimmed with red and her formerly rosy cheeks were blotchy.

"My father never would have left if it hadn't been super-important," she told Holly as they swept forward in the crowd, a crooked smile on her face.

"Oh, I know. I'm sure it was really important," Holly told her.

But not as important as you are.

chapter eleven

After seven months in school, it was apparent to Holly Faye that she was never going to meet a boy as gentle as Tyler. So they decided to get married. She wore a flowing gown whose train was as long as she was tall. Ditz played the piano, and her mother sat in the first pew of the church, weeping.

At least Holly thought she heard weeping. No, it was a ringing telephone.

Her ringing telephone.

It awakened Holly from her dream.

"You've got to come and get me!" cried the voice when she clicked on.

"What? Ditz?" Holly mumbled, sitting upright in her bed. She was in that haze between sleeping and waking up. Her clock said 2:14 A.M.

"Wake up!" Ditz practically yelled over the telephone. "I'm out here in the middle of nowhere, and the creep took my purse. Thank God I've got my cell phone. Take the three twenties that are in that little porcelain box on my nightstand."

"What creep?" Holly said hazily. "Where did you say you were?" It was too much too quickly for someone who'd been sound asleep. She and her choral group had returned from a concert in Tupelo right before midnight. They had sung hard during the show, and harder on the bus, so much so that Holly had gone to bed with no thought to the fact that Ditz wasn't in hers.

"I'll tell you later. Listen." Ditz spoke more slowly this time, and Holly could hear a truck going by. "You need to come and get me."

"How? I don't know how to drive," Holly said, her mind all muddy water.

"Walk behind the school and over the hill to Seventh and Blanchard," Ditz said. "Nobody will see you go out the back door. Nobody will use it until the kitchen people come in. Call a taxi now, and have it meet you at that corner. Tell the driver to take you to the Redeye Saloon. I'm about a half mile down the road from there. East, I think. Okay?"

"Uh . . . okay."

"Hurry!" Dial tone.

Holly dialed directory assistance and, once she'd been connected, asked the taxi dis-

patcher to have a car meet her in ten minutes
at Seventh and Blanchard. Then she pulled on a
pair of jeans, a gift from Ditz, over the Norwood's Auto Body and Repair T-shirt in which
she slept, and grabbed her jacket. Just like Ditz
had said, she found three twenties.

Surely that would be enough to get her to
the Redeye Saloon, but what about getting
home? She scrounged through her own dresser
and came up with seven more bucks. On a wing
and a prayer, she was off.

Her heart was pounding as she snuck out
the back door and hurried across the campus.
She was sure there were boogeymen behind
every tree, and by the time she saw the lights of
the waiting cab, she was practically in tears.

"You got money?" the greasy-haired driver
asked suspiciously when she got in. "It's fifteen
bucks out to the Redeye."

Holly waved a twenty at him. "Yes. Please

hurry." She'd never been in a taxi, and she was glad he didn't ask her anything else. As they approached the Redeye Saloon, Holly asked him to slow down. A few seconds later she spotted a girl in the shadows of the road.

"Over there!" she cried as Ditz flagged them down with her cell phone.

Holly had never been so happy to see someone in her life. Ditz slid in beside her, her teeth chattering from the cold March air. She was wearing a short lacey blue dress and matching sweater. Her long brown hair was blown every which way, her panty hose had a run, and her sweater was buttoned up wrong. To top it off, she smelled like a smokestack.

"Take us back to Haverty, please," Holly told the driver.

"You didn't tell me we were picking someone up. There's a five-dollar surcharge after midnight."

"We'll pay it," Ditz said, sinking back on the ripped vinyl seat and kicking off her heels. The taxi made a U-turn.

"Spill," Holly ordered.

Ditz took a big breath. "Remember that guy I told you about, Kevin? The one I met last week outside the movie theater in Hattiesburg?"

Holly nodded.

"He called and asked if I wanted to go out tonight. We had a real nice dinner at this bar-becue place and then we came over to the Red-eye and had a few cocktails, and—"

"How many?"

Ditz shrugged. "Three or four."

"Three or four."

"I'm not going to tell you if you're going to give me a hard time!" Ditz threatened.

Holly waited.

Ditz took another breath. "We had just got-ten back into his car and were going home when he started kissing me and touching me and pawing me like a sheep at a shearing." She made a face. "At first I didn't mind it, but then he was all wet and slobbery and he belched right in my face."

"Gross!" Holly wrinkled her nose.

"I told him to stop, and he didn't, and I slapped him but good."

Holly sucked in her cheeks. "Then what?"

"Then he tells me that'll be the last time I ever touch him and he opens the door, shoves me out, and drives away with my purse still in the car!" Ditz shook her cell phone in anger. "The bouncer at the Redeye wouldn't let me back in without my ID, and I didn't like the look of some of the guys hanging around outside, so I decided I'd pretend like I was going to meet my boyfriend."

"And that's when you called me?"

Ditz's blue eyes looked sheepish. "Not

exactly. The squeal of Kevin's tires as he pulled out of the parking lot caught the attention of some policemen patrolling the Redeye. One cop car took off after him and the other pulled up by me."

"If they found out how young you were you could have been arrested!" Holly exclaimed.

Ditz waved her comment away. "I told the officer what had happened, and he asked me how old I was. I told him I was old enough." She laughed wickedly.

"Ditz!"

"Hey, he was pretty darn cute. I could tell I was getting to him. I told *him* he was cute and I gave him my, well our, telephone number, and said I was waiting for my brother to come and get me. That's when he let me go. And *that's* when I snuck into the cattails over there by the roadside and called you."

"You gave him what?" Holly yelled so loudly

the cabdriver spun around and glared at her.
She couldn't believe her ears.

"Oh, don't worry, I wouldn't *really* give a
cop our real number, even if he did look like
a movie star." Ditz yawned, closing her eyes.
"Man. All of a sudden I am totally exhausted."

After shelling out the cab fare and getting
Ditz safely back to their dorm room, Holly
flipped on the small dresser lamp. Ditz
groaned at the sight of herself in the entry-
way mirror.

"I need to pee and sleep in a major way,"
she said, stumbling into the bathroom. When
she came out and crawled into bed with her
clothes on, Holly covered her with a blanket
and turned out the light.

Holly was awakened at dawn by the sounds
of dry heaving coming from the bathroom. Ditz
must not have had time to close the bathroom
door. Still wearing the clothes she'd had on the

night before, she sat on the floor, her head over the commode.

Drinking is so glamorous, thought Holly. She put on some clothes, went down to the cafeteria, and picked up a couple of English muffins and two cups of coffee. She got their mail too.

There were the usual campus flyers, a letter from Tyler, and assorted catalogs for clothing and bath products and record clubs. Those were all addressed to Ms. Lydia Hale, King Dormitory.

And so was the long, cream-colored envelope from the Haverty Student Review Board.

"Hi, Mom," Ditz said with false cheer, pacing back and forth in their dorm room. She'd changed into jeans and a sweater, and her hair was wet from the shower. "Nothing's wrong! Can't I call you just to say hi?"

Holly's jaw dropped. "Slight exaggeration," she mouthed.

After sitting like a zombie for the past two hours, the letter in her lap, Ditz had left a message with Dr. McSpadden's secretary begging him not to inform her parents of her current situation. She had promised both him and Holly that she would discuss everything with her mom when they got together in St. John's over spring break, and that she really, really, *really* would focus on her studies.

Then she'd called her house, but Magdalena had said her father was at the gym and her mom was at brunch. So Ditz had called her mom on her cell.

Why is she acting like everything is okay? Holly worried, watching Ditz clutch the phone. If there was anyone she should be coming clean to, it was her mom. What was the point of calling if she didn't?

Holly watched as Ditz's face clouded over. "What do you mean, we aren't going to St. John's? But we've been planning on it since before New Year's," she wailed. "You promised we'd have some time—yes, I know, but—I know, but—"

All of a sudden Holly wished she had excused herself before Ditz had phoned home.

"Fine. Whatever." Ditz was scowling now. "Mom, I don't *care* that they've got a great teen program at that place in Florida. I don't *want* to go back there. I wanted to go to St. John's." Her hands were shaking. "With you," she half whispered.

Holly was planning on spending spring break in sunny Biscay, but she knew that a lot of the students traveled to Florida, or even to an island in the tropics, like Ditz. *Guess Ditz won't be one of them this year,* she thought somberly.

Ditz's voice took on new vigor. "Actually, there were a few things I did want to talk to you about now. I got my purse stolen last night. I was—" She frowned. "No, it wasn't my Fendi. I—yes, I already phoned the credit card company. I didn't have anything else in there worth anything. Except my fake ID," she blurted out, startling Holly with her boldness.

Obviously that news sailed right over Mrs. Hale's head, because Ditz skipped on to the next item. "Mom, the school sent me a letter. They said—they said I need to improve my grades."

Yes! Holly gave her a thumbs-up.

"No, it wasn't from Dr. McSpadden. It was from the Student Review Board." Ditz listened for a moment. "I don't know. I guess because they're the ones who do this sort of thing." She listened some more, and her face grew stony. "Okay, Mother. I know you'll pull all the right strings," she said flatly. "You're right. I won't worry. And

I—" She stared at the receiver. "Mom? Hello? Are you there?" A few seconds passed. "Oh, the mimosas and omelets just arrived for you and Whitney. Okay. Mm-hmm. Bye."

Ditz couldn't even look at Holly as she placed the phone back in its cradle.

"Ditz?" Holly said, touching her friend gently on the arm. "If you don't have plans for spring break, there's someplace I'd be happy to have you visit."

"So this is where you grew up," Ditz said enthusiastically as they got off the bus and walked down the path to the Lovells' house a few weeks later.

Holly had to smile at her friend's reaction. "This is it." She pointed to the small woodsy area across the street. "That's where my friends and I used to play hide-and-seek—there's some great hiding places in there. If you head in the opposite direction, you'll run into Norwood's Auto Body and Repair." She couldn't wait to show Tyler off to Ditz on his home turf.

"And up there beyond that big old elm tree—that's my house."

The small yellow ranch with the neat flower beds and green plastic mailbox that read LOVELL, W suddenly looked much smaller and plainer now that Holly was with Ditz. Holly had seen pictures of Ditz's house, a massive brick colonial with a circular driveway. As she pushed open her own house's back screen door and stepped inside, the house felt smaller too, the cracked linoleum looming up to meet them and the framed prints of overalls-wearing teddy bears on the walls looking pathetic.

Holly turned to Ditz, an apologetic expression on her face. "I know it's not much—"

"It's just like a dollhouse!" Ditz exclaimed,

putting down her duffel bag and stretching her arms. "It's adorable!"

"And you're just as pretty as Holly Faye said you were," said Wanda, hurrying out from her room. "You must be Lydia!" Princess came running out too, yapping at Wanda's slippered heels and barking as ferociously as a toy poodle could.

"Oh, he's so cute!" Ditz breathed as Holly picked up Princess and kissed her soft apricot-colored fur. Then Ditz turned with a smile to Wanda. "Please, Mrs. Lovell, call me Ditz—and wait, I already know you're going to give me a hard time about that!"

Holly had worried about what Ditz would think of her mother's birthmark.

She needn't have. Ditz was so warm and friendly it was as if it weren't even there.

Wanda shook her head, laughing. "I can't believe a girl as pretty as you could have such a silly name . . . but if you say so, Ditz it is. On one condition. You call me Wanda." She hugged Holly and a yelping Princess tight. "Welcome home, honeybun. A whole week with you! Princess and I will be on cloud nine." Then she reached out and pulled Ditz into their embrace. "We'll make this the best spring break ever."

Holly had told her mom a little bit about Ditz's family situation. She knew her mom would keep her reaction to herself.

"I'm so glad I get to meet you. Thank you so much for having me. I felt so bad that you couldn't join us on Parents' Weekend," Ditz told Wanda as she looked around the house, seeming to drink everything in.

Holly didn't think she'd ever forget the expression on her mom's face as Wanda's eyes met her own. "You—you remember, Mom," she stammered out, willing her mom to go along with her. "All those . . . those alterations you had to do."

"Parents' Weekend," Wanda said after a slight pause. She looked like she'd been slapped. Ditz might have thought it was because of regret over the missed weekend, but Holly knew better. "Oh, yes. I—I just was so snowed under with work that I couldn't go."

The lump in Holly's throat was almost too painful to swallow.

Wanda changed the subject quickly. "Do you girls want something to drink? I just made a pitcher of pink lemonade."

Holly was relieved even as she felt guilty. Yes, they'd have some pink lemonade.

Spring break in Biscay flew by faster than a hummingbird's wings. Holly made sure to introduce Ditz to all the people she'd heard about from Wanda's letters. They took Princess for long walks and swapped boyfriend stories with Bel, visited with the women at the quilting bee (now at work on a Victorian-style crazy quilt, piecing together treasured keepsake fabrics), peeked in at Ethlyn Chall and her poodle perm (still as frizzy as ever), and had a shampoo and blow-dry at Juanita's Shear Magic Salon (on the house).

After meeting him on one of his visits to Haverty, Ditz already thought Tyler was the dreamiest boy on the planet. Now, seeing him fiddling around with the old T-bird his daddy was restoring, she promised not to fall in love with him but threatened to put up an ad for a Tyler clone.

"I need to find me a good old boy," she fussed to Holly one night after Tyler had gone home.

"If we stay here long enough, you just

might," Holly countered. Glamorous Ditz had all the boys in Biscay lining up just to get a glimpse.

On Sunday Holly, Ditz, and Wanda went to church, where Holly sang a solo so beautiful that many of the adults, including grown men, had tears in their eyes.

It rained like cats and dogs that afternoon. Wanda declared it was high time they stop gallivanting all over town, make a pot of tea, and put their feet up.

"I suppose I should do some reading for world lit class," Ditz said with a sigh, pulling a copy of *Jane Eyre* from her backpack as she plopped onto the Lovells' couch. Then she tossed the novel on the floor. "Oh, who am I fooling? I just want to sit here and shoot the breeze with y'all." Her mouth curved down. "Tomorrow's our last day here."

Holly had hoped Ditz would understand

that she was from a humble situation and that she could like Biscay—she'd never expected her to *love* it.

Holly's own eyes had been opened. She had been proud of her hometown, but seeing it through Ditz's eyes had made everything new again. And it turned out that Biscay, with its down-home characters and wide open spaces, was a lot cooler than she'd ever realized.

"Can I ask you Lovell women something?" Ditz was looking at them, a sheepish expression on her face.

"Of course," Wanda said, putting down the embroidered pillow sham she was working on.

She's going to ask about the birthmark, Holly thought, wincing. Sooner or later, everyone did.

"Please don't take this the wrong way." Ditz looked like she was gathering courage. "I've been in a lot of houses, houses with antique furniture and media rooms and built-in pools

. . . and sometimes the people who live there are miserable. But you—you live in a house that's, well . . . modest. And you're about the happiest family I've ever met." She hesitated. "I hope I'm not insulting you or anything."

Wanda nodded encouragingly. "Of course not. Go on, sweetie."

"See, me, I'm . . . I'm *one* of those people who lives in a big house with antique furniture so old it should be in a museum." She laughed hollowly. "Any movie you want to watch, we have on DVD. Our cook makes me breakfast every day when I'm home. And our pool is better than the one at my dad's country club." Her shoulders sagged. "But I'm . . . I'm not happy."

Holly's heart went out to her. The drinking, the casual way Ditz hooked up with boys, the partying. You didn't do those things if you were really happy inside.

"I know it must seem strange to you that we're content with so little," Wanda told Ditz as Holly, not sure how content *she* really was, looked self-consciously up at the homemade curtains.

"Strange?" To Holly's surprise, Ditz laughed. "Not at all. I see why you're happy. You've got great friends, wonderful home-cooked meals, and the coziest, snuggest place I've ever slept in."

Ditz looked as if she were searching for the right words. "Don't get me wrong. I don't want any pity because I'm no poor little rich girl, honest. I love a great pair of designer shoes and the prospect of getting a Beemer on my sixteenth birthday just like the next girl. But I always think stuff is going to make me happy, and it doesn't. And after staying here with you . . ." She trailed off. "Is it hopeless for me?"

"Hopeless?" Wanda shook her head, smiling. "Your life's spiritual journey is just beginning."

Ditz hunched her shoulders. "But see, I'm not spiritual at all. I'm not into going to church every week. That's not to say I didn't love going with y'all today," she said quickly, backtracking. "But it's really not for me. The church we belong to in Nashville is filled with some of the snootiest people I've ever met."

"The house of the Lord doesn't filter out the flock," Wanda agreed. "But being spiritual doesn't mean you need to go to church every Sunday. Take me, for example. Most weeks you'll find me dressed in my Sunday best sitting in the fourth pew from the back. But I don't need to go to church to talk to God. Sometimes I talk to him right here in my house. When I'm in the kitchen, or working on a project. Being spiritual means being true to yourself. True to how you want to live your life."

. . . .

"I know it might not seem like it, the way I carry on sometimes," Ditz said, looking shamefaced at Holly, "but I really respect you and your values. You're always honest, and you work so hard. Sometimes I've wondered how you do it." She laughed lightly. "Haverty's got lots of other good girls, I guess, but until I met Holly, well—Haverty seemed filled with plenty of snobs that'd knock you down." Then she gazed over at Wanda. "Now, after coming here, I know."

A tremor of guilt shot through Holly. She wasn't as good or as kind as Ditz thought she was. She *was* a hard worker, and she always *wanted* to do the right thing, even if it didn't always turn out that way. But hadn't she been embarrassed about her mom? About where she came from? A flush spread across her cheeks.

"See, there you go getting embarrassed. You

just can't take any praise," Ditz jokingly repri-
manded her.

"I'm not as good as you think I am," Holly
said softly, not looking at Ditz or her mom.
Maybe her life's spiritual journey was just beginning too? Maybe it wasn't too late to start
appreciating her mom and everything she had
done for her.

Wanda got out of her chair, came over, and
clasped Ditz's hand. "Sweetie, everyone, no
matter how rich or how poor, faces obstacles,
whether they be people or situations or physi-
cal limitations. You just have to find your own
way to deal with them. I've always had to strug-
gle with money, and having this birthmark on
my face made me change—not how I felt about
myself, but how I viewed others. It's been a
blessing, in many, many ways.

"And when I have a problem, well, I never
feel taller than when I'm on my knees. But

that's just me. I'm fortunate to have so many good friends, friends that have become family." For a split second an emotion passed across Wanda's face that Holly couldn't read. Then it smoothed over, and she smiled at Holly. "And the world's most wonderful daughter."

chapter twelve

"I promise I'll bring you back a slice," Ditz said as she and Ruby walked out onto the porch.

"A slice? I want the whole pie!" Holly called after her, laughing. Ditz had fallen in love with Ruby's toasted almond torte, and Ruby had invited her to visit her at her house and learn how to make it. Ditz had been thrilled, and since today was their last one in Biscay, it gave Holly some time alone with Wanda.

But considering how her mom was acting, Holly wasn't sure if this was a good idea or not. Her normally calm mother had been fidgety and jumpy all morning. When Princess barked at a passing delivery truck, a startled Wanda had dropped a glass on the floor. She'd poked herself twice with her needle. She'd whispered something to Ruby, after which Ruby had hugged her and told her it would all work out. And Wanda kept staring at Holly, then quickly looking away. It was all very strange.

Holly couldn't figure it out. And after Ditz left and her mom asked her to come sit down at the dining room table—a table usually reserved for Easter, Thanksgiving, Christmas, and birthday celebrations, Holly was downright alarmed.

"Mom, what is it?" Holly asked as her mom sat down across from her, her folded hands clasped tightly on the table. "I know you're probably mad about Parents' Weekend, as well as being sad about my going back, but I promise I'll be home soon." And she would. This visit had made her realize how important her relationship with her mom really was. How important it was that they spend time together.

"That's not it." Wanda looked as if she were steeling herself for a blow of some kind. "I can't deny I wasn't hurt about Parents' Weekend, but that's not what I need to tell you. I've kept something from you, Holly Faye. I've been afraid to tell you, but I can't let it go on any longer. You have a right to know."

Holly didn't like the sound of this. Whatever could be making her mom's tone so grave?

"Fifteen years ago there was a terrible fire in a group of row houses at the edge of Biscay. A fire that killed nineteen people."

Holly relaxed a little. "Shoot, Mom. I know about the fire." Everyone in Biscay did, although the grown-ups never seemed to want to talk about it much. "Is that what you're making such a big deal about? That dumb old fire?"

Her mother swallowed. "Let me finish. You might think we've had things hard, but when I was in my twenties, times were even rougher. I didn't get on too well with my folks, and I won't go into those details, but we parted ways. I rented a small apartment on the other side of town. I'd just gotten out of a bad relationship, and I'd been working as a waitress over at the Haverty Diner, mostly nights. One Friday tips were bad, and I couldn't afford the bus fare home. So I walked. That was the very night when I saw the flames."

"You saw the fire?" Holly asked, trying to imagine how horrible it must have been.

"I was the first one on the scene. The flames were shooting out and the air was filled with smoke. And fear. I could hear the screams coming from inside, and I watched in terror as people bashed out windows, trying to escape."

"Oh, Mom," Holly whispered, taking her hand.

"Through the smoke I could see a woman on the second floor, coughing and heaving. She was screaming something, and I tried to make out what it was. 'Baby,' she choked out. 'Baby.'"

A tight coil of fear wound its way through Holly's stomach.

"Then what?" she whispered.

"It was like—like an angel was calling me. Because right then, amid all the screaming and the blazing and the hot ashes raining down around me, I heard the cry—the cry of that baby." Wanda blinked back tears. "There was only one thing I could do. I ran inside. And although I tried to shield my face from the flames, something inside me just propelled me through the smoke and fire."

By now Holly was sobbing. All of a sudden

she knew what her mom was going to tell her, knew that—

"That baby, wrapped snug in a blanket, was sitting in a bassinet—warm, yes, but amazingly unharmed. The woman had tried to come downstairs, but she had passed out on the steps. I couldn't budge her. Coughing and choking, I snatched up the baby and ran through the blazing building to safety. I must have blacked out when I got outside. The next thing I knew, I was in the hospital over in Natchez, and Juanita and Ruby and her husband, Gordon—he was still living, bless his soul—were by my side."

I'm adopted. I'm adopted! "It's amazing that you didn't get burned," Holly cried. "You must have been—"

"But I did, Holly." Wanda lifted shaking fingers to touch her birthmark.

Oh, dear Lord. Her birthmark . . .

Wanda cleared her throat. "I had to stay in the hospital for a week, and the staff cared for you and treated you as if you were one of their own."

Holly could hardly find her voice. "But what about—"

As if she could read her mind, Wanda began to cry. "Your birth parents died, Holly Faye. No one survived the Biscay fire. No one except . . . except you." Her shoulders were racked with sobs. "Oh, Holly Faye, please forgive me. I should have told you sooner."

"Then your face . . . it's not a birthmark after all," Holly said slowly, her mind still trying to grasp what her mom was saying.

"But it is," Wanda said, gazing into her watery eyes. "It *is* a birthmark. As I took you from the fire, a flame branded me for life. I was reborn and became a loving mother the moment I held you in my arms."

Neither of them spoke for a long moment. Finally Holly did. "But how did—I mean why— why did they let you keep me? Aren't there courts and laws and things? Didn't anyone else come forward to claim me?"

"No one did. The fire was publicized nationwide, and surely if your birth parents had had any kin they would have stepped forward. When no one claimed you, the state said they would place you in an orphanage. Of course I couldn't let them do that. Ruby's husband found me a lawyer from Hub City, and he represented me in the court case." Wanda rubbed a hand across her eyes. "Thankfully we had a sympathetic judge, who decided that although I was single and not well-to-do, you'd be better off with one healthy, hardworking parent than in an orphanage."

It was so hard to comprehend. She was an orphan. *Just like Mrs. Hale said.*

"Juanita and Ruby found a church-run home for single mothers that I went to for a spell. When I came home three months later with a healthy baby girl, there were some whispered rumors and snide glares at the grocery store, but it soon died out. Everyone assumed they knew what had happened, and we didn't make them any the wiser."

"So Juanita and Ruby . . . they know?" Holly said, incredulous at the friendship they had shown her family.

"Yes, honey. The entire quilting circle knows. They swore when you were an infant to never breathe a syllable, and they've been true to their word. And they have been after me for a long time to tell you the truth." Wanda walked unsteadily to the sideboard and took a tattered scrapbook from the drawer. "I kept all the clippings from the paper about the fire, as well as the documents from the court case. It's all here, whenever you want to read it."

"My birthday," Holly said suddenly, gazing up at her mom. "How do you know my birthday was on Christmas Eve?"

"The doctors guessed you were about a month old when I rescued you that horrible January night. We decided there could be no greater gift than a baby, and when I had to fill in your birthday on some documents, I didn't hesitate to say you came on Christmas Eve."

Numb, Holly gripped the table.

"There's one more thing," her mom said, her voice catching. "The pearls—the pearl necklace I gave you?"

"Yes?" Holly had almost forgotten about it—the box was in her dresser drawer back at school.

"When the nurses at the hospital took you out of your blanket, they found the box at your feet, tucked under the folds of your cotton gown." Wanda let out a half-sob. "It was as if your mama wanted to provide for you in some way. I lied when I told you I got them at Gower's, Holly. They're real pearls. And they're worth a lot of money."

Holly let out a strangled cry. *My birth mom and dad died . . . the person I thought was my mom isn't . . . I almost died in a fire and was rescued by the bravest woman in the world . . . I was adopted . . . whispered rumors . . . the birthmark . . . the scar . . . the pearls . . . real . . . Haverty . . . embarrassment . . . she loves me . . . she loves me . . . she loves me . . .* It was all too much.

Choking down tears, Holly pushed back her chair and fled to her room, her mind spinning and her heart squeezing with love and pain over what she had just heard.

She didn't know that her mom's heart was squeezing just as hard.

When Holly and Ditz left for the bus back to Haverty, Ditz couldn't hug Wanda enough, and didn't even seem to notice the odd farewell between Holly and her mom.

April 6

Dear Diary,

I've done it. I've broken her heart.

And mine too.

When she kissed me good-bye before she took the bus, I just didn't know what more to say. Lord, you gave me the strength, now help me keep my faith that I have a beloved daughter forever.

As the bus rolled away from Biscay, Holly wiped a stray tear from her cheeks.

"Sure, you're sad to leave, but you'll see your mom soon," Ditz reassured her, patting her arm. That's when Holly told Ditz everything.

"Wow," Ditz said at last, her eyes clear blue saucers. Then, once more, "Wow."

The tears just kept falling, no matter how much she tried to keep it together. The amazing story of her life was still so fresh and raw that it hurt every time she said the words.

"I can't believe I'm adopted," Holly whispered as the bus traveled down the highway. "That my mom is not . . . my mom."

Ditz put her arm around Holly. "Are you kidding me? She is too your mom. You and she have an amazing relationship, even if you don't have the same genes." A wry smile appeared on her lips. "I have my mom's nose and my dad's big feet, so I know there's no way I'm adopted. And how do I get along with them? I don't." She straightened her shoulders. "But after talking with your mom, I'm going to try to change that. I'm going to be honest with them and tell them how I feel." She stared out the window.

"Whether you're adopted or not doesn't make any difference when you've got love in your heart."

"But what's in my heart has been horrible!" Holly burst out, making a few passengers turn around in their seats. "I've been so ashamed of people seeing my mom, seeing that ugly red birthmark—and it turns out that she got that birthmark by saving my life. I *caused* her to have that scar, Ditz. It's all my fault." Fresh tears began to fall. Holly was just so angry with herself. *How could I have been ashamed of my mom? She's always loved me more than anything in the world.* Wanda had risked her own life to take in a child who had no one.

A little orphan scholarship girl.

"Do you love her?" Ditz asked gently.

"More than I ever knew," Holly sobbed, not caring how pitiful she looked.

Ditz reached into her bag and handed Holly

a tissue. "Okay, then. We're gonna come up with something that proves it to her. Something she'll never forget."

"Like what?" Holly sniffled.

Ditz was silent for a few seconds. Then she snapped her fingers. "The annual Haverty Mother's Day performance. Oh, it's always a big deal. They film it live for *The Haverty Talent Hour,* and Frank Shepherd always makes it a point to do something bigger and better than they did the previous year. Something no one's ever done before . . . "

A gleam appeared in Ditz's eyes. "Something like having a sophomore sing. Of course, she'd have to have an amazing multioctave voice."

Holly's breath caught in her throat. "Do you think there's a chance—"

"What good are having strings to pull unless you give 'em a tug every now and then?" Ditz said, grinning as she whipped out her cell phone. "Yes. I'd like the number for Dr. McSpadden's office at the Haverty School of Music," she said importantly into the receiver. Holly fell back in her seat, the whirl of the day's emotions fluttering like a songbird in her heart.

chapter thirteen

"Live, from the Haverty School of Music and the Performing Arts in Hattiesburg, Mississippi, it's *The Haverty Talent Hour,* a one-hour recital that features the best young musicians at the best school of music in the South. Tonight's performance is a special one, honoring all the wonderful mothers in this land of ours. And now . . . on with the show!" A girl stepped to the microphone and began to play a classical flute piece as Frank Shepherd hustled offstage.

Holly stood in the wings, trying to calm her already frayed nerves. Tonight, for the first time in the twenty-five-year history of *The Haverty Talent Hour,* a Haverty sophomore would be singing—and on the Mother's Day program, no less.

Holly Faye Lovell.

After Ditz had pulled her strings and Holly had secured nominations from her instructors, Holly had been summoned to the television producers' office, where she auditioned. Not only had the decision to include her in the Mother's Day performance been unanimous, but they had decided she would close the show.

Ditz had taken her shopping for the most incredible dress she'd ever laid eyes on. It was a beautiful deep peach shantung, with a form-fitting bodice and a frothy tulle skirt. Holly's jaw had dropped when the clerk in the boutique had rung it up, but Ditz hadn't batted an eye. "This is nothing compared to all you've done for me," she'd said with obvious delight. Then there had been the shoes and the stockings and the earrings . . . and the bracelet from Tyler and Holly's own pearls.

Now Ditz was sitting in the audience with Wanda, Juanita, Ruby, Annabel, and Tyler, waiting for Holly to perform. Butterflies zoomed through Holly's stomach as she thought of all the people sitting out there, and of the six special people who meant so very much to her.

For a while Holly got caught up in the performances, her heart lifting at the sound of one boy's violin, her toe tapping to another's fiddle playing. Then, before she could blink, it was her turn.

"Ready?" mouthed her voice coach, Natalie Edwards.

"Ready," Holly mouthed back. *Lord, please let me use my voice as you intended. And please, let me make my mom and those that I love proud.*

Squaring her shoulders and taking a deep breath, Holly walked steadily across the Haverty stage, just as she'd watched so many performers do.

"Good evening," she said, her voice clear and confident. "My name is Holly Faye Lovell and I'm from Biscay, Mississippi. Tonight I'll be singing 'The Wind Beneath My Wings.' I'd like to dedicate it to my mother, Wanda Jo."

As the orchestra began to play, Holly sang the first words of the song, one of her favorites. The words were familiar friends, and she warmed to them, her voice punching each note lightly.

Memories of other days and other songs

filled her mind. Singing with her mom in the bathtub when she was a toddler . . . crooning on their porch swing . . . humming in the car . . . harmonizing in the backyard on a moonlit summer night.

Musical memories that made her heart ache for all the love her mother had for her, all that she had given for her.

The orchestra swelled behind her.

"'Did I ever tell you you're my hero?'" Holly sang, finding her mother in the crowd. Her voice deepened and then went higher, rising and soaring. The music coursed through her veins, its message so true, the melody so beautiful.

Ditz had said they needed to come up with something that would prove how much Holly loved Wanda. Something Wanda would never forget.

And as Holly's voice soared into the Mississippi May sky, she knew she'd hit the jackpot.

When she was through, the crowd burst into applause. They gave her a standing ovation. Holly had had no idea an audience could applaud so loudly. There was a moment, a single moment, when the clapping seemed to shake the solid, stately walls that had stood for a century.

Holly's nerves almost crumbled when Frank Shepherd walked toward her. This was big stuff. Frank Shepherd never talked to you unless he thought you were really something. Only the very best performers on *The Haverty Talent Hour* got the chance to chat with him onstage afterward.

She tried to look as normal as a fifteen-year-old could who had just made her television debut and was still standing.

"That was one of the most outstanding

performances we have ever witnessed here on the Haverty stage!" Frank Shepherd boomed, taking her shaking hands in his. "Is this a winsome young lady or what?" he asked the studio audience, who cheered some more.

Holly hoped her knees wouldn't buckle as the cameraman zoomed in for a close-up. "Thank you, Mr. Shepherd."

Frank Shepherd pointed to the strand of pearls lying snug around her neck. "Now, was that lovely necklace a gift for this special occasion? After all," he said, turning to the audience with genuine astonishment, "Holly Faye Lovell is the youngest person ever to perform on *The Haverty Talent Hour*."

Another outpouring of wild applause.

Holly searched the crowd, blinking under the bright lights until she found Wanda once more. "These pearls are a gift from my mom." *Both of my moms.*

Frank Shepherd looked pleased that he'd guessed correctly.

Holly took a deep, steadying breath. "And I know that they're expensive, but they aren't the biggest or most important gift I've received. The biggest gift is the gift of love . . . and of life.

"Everybody has a mother," Holly told the audience. "And I suppose everybody hopes and wants theirs to be the best, but mine really is. Really. I love you, Mom," she choked out, wiping the tears from her cheeks.

Frank Shepherd cleared his throat. "Holly Faye, you are one extraordinary girl. I think it's only right that, seeing as this is our Mother's Day special, Ms. Wanda Lovell join her beautiful daughter here on the stage."

An usher escorted a shaking Wanda up the steps and into Holly's arms. The audience loved it. Holly hugged her mom and Wanda hugged back.

. . . .

And as the camera zoomed in for a closing shot, Holly knew that the lens had captured the right side of Wanda's face, the side with the birthmark. But it didn't matter, because after all, that birthmark was what made her mother the most beautiful woman in the world.

Love is the language of the heart all over the world, but especially in small Southern towns. Biscay, Mississippi, is no exception. Love drifts through the houses in heartfelt hugs and kisses, and it floats across flower-strewn meadows and shimmering lakes. In Biscay, love makes the world go round.

Because people are people, with hopes and dreams and faith in their hearts and stars in their eyes . . . especially those who were born in Biscay, Mississippi.

about the authors

Besides being an author, **Britney** is that rare phenomenon, a megastar—one who still phones her mom every night, no matter where she is. Not only is Britney the bestselling female artist during any one-week period in music history, but her debut album, . . . *Baby One More Time,* made her the youngest artist to hit the 10-million mark. Her second album, *Oops! . . . I Did It Again,* sold more than 1.3 million copies in its first week and to date has sold more than 17 million CDs worldwide.

Besides being the mother of the planet's biggest superstar, **Lynne** taught school in Kentwood, Louisiana, for several years before taking time off to be her daughter's biggest fan. She and her husband, Jamie, are the parents of Bryan, Britney, and Jamie Lynn Spears.

$\mathcal{B}$ritney Spears has created The Britney Spears Foundation, a charitable foundation formed with The Giving Back Fund, a national nonprofit organization that helps professional athletes, entertainers, and others establish and maintain charitable foundations for philanthropic giving.

As part of this effort, The Britney Spears Foundation funds and operates a performing arts camp for over 100 economically disadvantaged boys and girls ages eleven to fourteen from New England and New York. The camp provides an intensive experience for campers to explore and develop their talents and learn how to go about pursuing a career in the performing arts. The staff consists of experienced counselors and master teachers in

various performing arts specialties who are dedi-
cated to enriching the lives of children through the
arts—as is Britney, who has cheered the campers'
amazing talents from a front-row seat at the camp's
performance finale.

To donate to The Britney Spears Foundation:

BY CREDIT CARD

*Visa and MasterCard are accepted. Include the credit
card number, expiration date, your name as it appears
on the credit card, and the donation amount.*

Telephone: 001 617 557-9910
Fax: 001 617 973-9463

ONLINE

www.britneyspears.com